DOCTOR WHO AND THE
TENTH PLANET

DOCTOR WHO AND THE TENTH PLANET

Based on the BBC television serial by Kit Pedler and Gerry Davis by arrangement with the British Broadcasting corporation

GERRY DAVIS

A TARGET BOOK
published by
the Paperback Division of
W. H. ALLEN & Co. Ltd

A Target Book
Published in 1976
by the Paperback Division of W. H. Allen & Co. Ltd
A Howard & Wyndham Company
44 Hill Street, London W1X 8LB

Reprinted 1979
Reprinted 1980
Reprinted 1982

Printed in Great Britain

ISBN 0 426 11068 4

Contents

The Creation of the Cybermen

Centuries ago by our Earth time, a race of men on the far-distant planet of Telos sought immortality. They perfected the art of cybernetics—the reproduction of machine functions in human beings. As bodies became old and diseased, they were replaced limb by limb, with plastic and steel.

Finally, even the human circulation and nervous system were recreated, and brains replaced by computers. The first cybermen were born.

Their metal limbs gave them the strength of ten men, and their in-built respiratory system allowed them to live in the airless vacuum of space. They were immune to cold and heat, and immensely intelligent and resourceful. Their large, silver bodies became practically indestructible.

Their main impediment was one that only flesh and blood men would have recognised: they had no heart, no emotions, no feelings. They lived by the inexorable laws of pure logic. Love, hate, anger, even fear, were eliminated from their lives when the last flesh was replaced by plastic.

They achieved their immortality at a terrible price. They became dehumanised monsters. And, like human monsters down through all the ages of Earth, they became aware of the lack of love and feeling in their lives and substituted another goal—power!

Later, forced to leave Telos, the Cybermen took refuge on the long-lost sister planet of Earth ... Mondas.

I

The Space Tracking Station

The long low room housed three separate rows of control consoles and technicians and resembled Cape Kennedy Tracking Station in miniature. At one end, the interior of a space capsule had been projected on to a large screen. Two astronauts were seated at the capsule controls.

The scene is a familiar enough one to TV watchers —but the attentive viewer would have noticed that the Tracking Station's ceiling was a little lower than that of Houston or Cape Kennedy, and that more of the technicians wore uniforms.

What he would never have guessed—looking round at the flushed, sweating men, in their singlets and open-necked shirts—was that immediately above the ceiling lay six feet of ice, and above that, the blizzard-swept wastes of the snowy Antarctic: the tracking station, code name *Snowcap*, was situated almost exactly over the South Pole.

One of the consoles, slightly raised above the others, faced the three rows of technicians. Behind it sat the three men responsible for the safe operation of Space Tracking Station *Snowcap*: General Cutler, the American soldier in charge of the predominantly military installation; Dr Barclay, an Australian physicist; and Dyson, an Englishman and senior engineer of the base.

General Cutler, his immaculate uniform neatly buttoned, and wearing a collar and tie, was apparently

7

unaffected by the close atmosphere inside the tracking station. Tall, with close-cropped grey hair, a firm jaw line, small shrewd black eyes and a large, unlit cigar clamped firmly between his teeth, he easily dominated the other two men.

The voice of Wigner, Head of International Space Control, came over the loudspeaker system.

'We're now handing *Zeus Four* to Polar Base. Will you take control, please?'

Cutler glanced towards the left-hand console, and received a nod from the monitoring technician. He pulled the desk microphone towards him:

'Yeah, we have *Zeus Four*, thank you, Geneva.'

The engineer, Dyson, clicked open his desk mike:

'*Snowcap* to *Zeus Four*, over to local control channel J for Jack.'

On the big screen facing them, one of the two men in the space capsule turned his head slightly and raised his thumb. His voice came over the loud-speakers:

'Over to J for Jack—now.'

General Cutler leaned back and removed his cigar for a moment. He smiled.

'Good morning, gentlemen, you lucky fellas! Having a good time up there?'

The second astronaut, Schultz, turned his head towards the camera. 'Why don't you come up and join us, General?'

Cutler gestured with his cigar. 'And miss my skiing?'

There was a ripple of laughter among the technicians facing Cutler. The General liked his little jokes to be appreciated. The two astronauts in the capsule grinned at the camera. Cutler nodded—as if acknowledging the laughter—and stuck the cigar back between his teeth.

8

'O.K., Barclay,' he said. 'They're all yours.'

Dr Barclay turned to Dyson. 'Give Texas tracking the next orbital pattern.'

Dyson nodded and started to operate his desk transmitter. 'Will do.'

Barclay glanced up at the screen. '*Snowcap* to *Zeus Four, Zeus Four*, how do you read me?'

Again, the voice of the astronaut Schultz, sounding unnaturally high-pitched and squeaky in the weightless atmosphere, came over the loudspeaker. 'Loud and clear, *Snowcap*, loud and clear. Hey, we have a great view of your weather. How is it your end?'

'Really want to know?' Barclay grinned. 'There's an ice blizzard and a force sixteen wind. Repeat your velocity for ground check, please.'

The two astronauts were reclining in the narrow capsule. Immediately above their heads, a complex row of instruments clicked out a stream of necessary data and information as the capsule hurtled round the earth towards its re-entry window. Through the two round side ports, the long shaft of sunlight constantly changed position as the space craft sped around the globe.

Major Schultz, a round-faced cheerful-looking German–American of about forty, and the older of the two men, turned to his partner. 'Skiing he says!'

Williams, a tall, handsome American negro of about thirty, nodded briefly before clicking on the communications microphone again. 'Williams. Cosmic ray measurements are now complete. Are you ready to receive data?'

The voice of Dr Barclay came through on the console above Williams' head. 'Yes, go ahead.'

Williams glanced over to the computer read-out controls set slightly to the right of the capsule panel, and started to relay the measurements. Schultz eased

9

back in his seat and stretched his legs slightly in one of the approved isometric astronaut's exercises. It had been a good, if uneventful, flight. In another couple of hours the capsule would be sitting in the blue waters of the Pacific, waiting to be winched aboard the aircraft carrier. And after that: the pleasures of hot food, a bath, and a real bed . . .

A pleasant run-of-the-mill mission. For a moment, the veteran astronaut thought back to the tougher flights of the past when space flight still entailed unpredictable hazards. The good old days! Perhaps it was all becoming a little too easy!

Inside the TARDIS, Ben, the Cockney sailor, was having similar thoughts. The last three landings had been uneventful—even dull. No danger, no excitement—merely a landing on some uninhabited planet, lengthy rambles with the Doctor to collect specimens of plants and rocks, and then off again.

Worse still, the Doctor seemed to be ageing rapidly. He was beginning to stoop a little, and his absent-mindedness had increased to the point where he did not seem to recognise his two companions, frequently addressing them as Ian and Barbara, the names of his first two fellow space-travellers.

Just before their most recent landing Ben had turned to Polly and muttered: 'I tell you, Duchess, if it goes on like this, I'm slinging my hook next port of call. Don't mind a bit of agro, but when it comes to sitting around waiting for the Doctor all day—and then him never telling us what he's doing—I've had it!'

The two of them were looking up at the television monitor screen which showed the latest landing place of the TARDIS. It didn't look very promising: white landscape, grey sky, and a thick swirling curtain of snowflakes.

'You can't go out in that!' The old Doctor shook his long white hair and tapped his lapel nervously with his long fingers—a familiar habit of his. 'It's quite out of the question.'

Ben was normally a good natured and obedient member of the Doctor's little party. Polly even teased him by saying that he was too ready to jump to attention and salute when the Doctor told him to do something. On this occasion, however, Ben stood firm. He crossed his arms defiantly. 'If I don't get some shore leave now, I warn you, I'm quitting. I don't care where we land, or what age it's in. Next time you open those doors, I'm going to scarper.'

The Doctor looked impatiently at Polly, and waited for her reaction. By nature a kind man, the Doctor had grown irritable and dictatorial of late. He didn't like to be crossed by one of his companions.

'Well,' he said, looking at Polly, 'what about you?'

Polly smiled a little nervously: 'If you say we can't go out, then of course we can't. But it wouldn't do any harm, would it?'

The Doctor flung his hands up. 'Any harm!' He looked at the control board. 'With a gale force wind and a blizzard—plus a mean temperature of thirty below zero!' He glanced up at the screen again. 'I don't even know where we've landed, or in which period of time.'

Ben threw a quick glance at Polly as if to say, 'That's why he's cross. Lost again!'

In spite of his age, the Doctor had sharp eyes and seemed almost able to read their minds. He noticed Ben's glance, interpreted it, and sulkily turned away.

'Oh, very well.' He nodded towards the almost inexhaustible equipment room of the TARDIS. 'You'll

11

find some Polar furs in there. You'd better bring some for me. I suppose I shall have to go out with you. Ten yards away from the TARDIS in this sort of weather, and you'd be hopelessly lost.'

The Doctor's two young companions ran into the equipment room before he changed his mind. Within five minutes, clad awkwardly and heavily in fur parkas, leggings and fur caps with ear flaps, the three adventurers opened the door of the TARDIS and stepped out into the snow.

The wind had already piled up the snow around the small blue police telephone box, and Polly began to shiver violently. The extreme cold cut short their breath and burned their lungs; icy particles of snow stung their faces with thousands of tiny pin pricks.

Polly and the Doctor made little progress in the face of the driving wind, but Ben heaved himself forward, step by step, through the loose drifting snow. Suddenly he appeared to collapse on his knees.

'He's hurt!' shouted Polly, and tried to hurry towards him, the Doctor close behind.

But Ben was pointing excitedly to something he had found. Four squat, black chimneys protruded through a small mound of snow. The three time travellers bent over them and felt warm air against their cheeks, flowing up from below.

'Something's buried under here, Doc.' Ben was shouting against the shriek of the Polar wind, his face close to the Doctor's ear. 'What is it?'

Before the Doctor could answer, Polly squealed excitedly from the other side of the chimneys. The long black snout of a periscope, similar to those used on submarines, had appeared from under the snow!

'Look what's here!' she called excitedly. 'A periscope!'

She turned back to peer into the lens of the periscope. 'Do you think there could be a submarine down here?'

Meanwhile, the Doctor was thoughtfully scraping the snow from a square hatch which he had discovered to one side of the chimneys. Obviously a trap door—but leading where?

The thick-set sergeant on duty in the base guardroom below stared in disbelief at the monitor screen which relayed the picture taken by the periscope's camera. He rubbed his eyes, shook his head, and looked again. 'Tito. Hey, Tito, come over here will'ya!'

Against the far wall of the guardroom stood a couple of bunks on which the guards took it in turn to snatch a few moments' sleep or relaxation. On the lower one, the second guard, an Italian–American named Tito, was reading a comic.

'Yeah, what is it?' He couldn't take his eyes off the adventures of Captain Marvel, who was engaged in a life or death struggle with a marauding party of robots.

The American Sergeant was still staring at the screen.

'I can see people!'

The bored soldiers at the base often played jokes on each other. Tito had heard it all before.

'Sure, sure. Lot's of people, skiing out there.' He turned another page of his comic.

'One of them's a girl.'

The Italian dropped his comic, swung himself off the bunk, and ran over. The three other guards, who had been playing poker at a table by the door, dropped their cards and converged on the small monitor screen.

Polly's face filled the screen as she looked into the lens of the periscope.

'A real live girl!' Tito grabbed the handles of the periscope and turned it round slightly.

Outside, the day had brightened and the driving snow eased a little. The assembled men could just make out the outline of the TARDIS. 'That looks like some kind of hut!'

The Sergeant looked over Tito's shoulder, and came to a decision: 'We'd better investigate.' He turned to the other three men.

'Take your small arms.' He jerked his thumb over to the row of sub-machine guns which were ranged in a rack by the door. 'Get outside and bring them down here. Now get moving!'

The three men quickly swung into their parkas, zipped them up, snatched a gun each from the rack, and started climbing the exit ladder at the far end of the room.

The three time travellers had finished inspecting the periscope. Despite the thick furs, Polly was trying to keep warm by swinging her arms and stamping her feet in the snow.

'I ... th ... think my face is getting frostbitten,' she stuttered through chattering teeth. 'C ... Can't we go back now, Doctor?'

As usual, the Doctor's mind was elsewhere. He continued to examine the periscope. 'Some kind of base, I imagine, set under the ice.'

Ben looked at Polly, and then at the Doctor. 'She's had enough, Doc. She wants to go back inside the TARDIS.'

'Oh yes, of course. I'm sure we've all had enough ...'

He swung round to lead the way back to the TARDIS, and stopped abruptly. Unnoticed by the three of them the trap door had been opened, and ranged alongside it were the sinister figures of the three soldiers in hoods and snow goggles. Their machine guns were levelled. The leading soldier gestured back towards the open trap door with his weapon.

Polly huddled against Ben. 'What does he want us to do?' she whispered in his ear.

'Come quietly, I expect.'

2

Disaster in Space

'Get a move on!' The Sergeant, hands on hips, watched as the three time travellers climbed awkwardly down the ladder. 'Back against that wall.'

The sudden transition from the dark, cold Antarctic ice cap to the brilliantly lighted, over-heated guardroom was almost too much for Polly. Ben took her arm as she began to sway dizzily.

'My dear fellow,' said the Doctor, as he brushed himself down, 'there's really no need to shout at us.'

'Easy, nice an' easy!' drawled the American Sergeant as the Doctor removed his furs.

'I assure you we're not carrying any weapons.' The Doctor spoke irritably. 'We are never armed.'

'Yeah? Well, just who are you?'

The other guards now entered and slammed the trap door shut behind them. They stared incredulously as the three travellers slowly pulled off their cumbersome fur garments, and whistled when they caught sight of Polly's long slender legs.

'O.K.,' said the Sergeant, 'I'll ask again. Who are you and what are you doing here?'

Polly, feeling a little more human and a little less like a Polar bear, smiled at him: 'We've landed just above you, Sergeant.'

'Landed? What in?'

'Oh in a ...' She stopped, suddenly remembering the Doctor's warning to keep their business to themselves at all times. '... It's a sort of spaceship, actually.'

'You can knock off the gags,' replied the Sergeant. 'You've no business here. This is a military base. Out of bounds to all civilians.'

The Doctor stepped forward: 'Ah, we must apologise then. Perhaps you wouldn't mind telling me just where we are, my dear chap?'

There was a quick smile on the faces of the assembled men. The Sergeant leant back against the table and folded his arms.

'You're standing in the South Pole Base of International Space Command, and frankly, pop——'

'Doctor, if you don't mind.'

'O.K., Doctor, your story's gonna have to be awful good.'

The Doctor's two companions gazed at each other in excitement.

'You mean we're on Earth?' burst out Polly.

'You heard, Duchess—South Pole,' Ben reminded her.

'Then we're home at last!' cried Polly, clutching Ben round the neck.

The Sergeant gazed wearily from one to the other. 'Boy! Have we some right kooks here! Tito,' he nodded towards the Italian–American, 'get the CO will ya.'

The smile dropped from Tito's face as he backed away towards the door. 'He's not going to like this!'

'The CO?' queried the Doctor.

'Commanding Officer—Boss!' Ben whispered in the Doctor's ear.

Tito picked up the phone by the door and dialled the number. 'Hello, sir. Duty Guard Private Tito here. Could you give a message to the General, please?'

Ben noticed that the men around the table stiffened to attention at the mention of the name. Cutler was

17

obviously a man to be reckoned with. Ben began to feel a twinge of nervousness.

'Sir. I know that,' Tito explained into the telephone. 'But this is an emergency. Oh, I see. The General's not there. Can you tell me where he is then, sir?'

'I'm right here, Private.' Tito had not noticed the door behind him open, and the General enter.

The men in the room immediately snapped to attention. Cutler, his face impassive as always, took in the scene. The long black cigar was still clenched firmly between his even white teeth.

'What's it all about, Sergeant?'

The Sergeant saluted and hesitated for a moment.

'Well, sir ...'

'Who are these people?' Cutler snapped.

'They just appeared ... outside in the snow.' Cutler nodded. 'They came out of a ...' The American Sergeant looked embarrassed, 'a hut!'

Cutler slowly turned his gaze away from the three time travellers to look at the Sergeant. 'A hut?'

'Yes, sir. It just appeared. We haven't seen it there before, that is ...'

Tito nodded in excited agreement. 'That's right, General. That's just the way it happened.'

Still with the same impassive, almost threatening look, Cutler moved towards the three companions, and walked around them as if inspecting troops.

He stopped in front of Ben and took in the sailor's uniform. 'Who are you?'

Ben snapped to attention, saluted: 'Able Seaman ... Ben Jackson ... sir. Royal Navy.'

'Then why aren't you with your ship?'

'Well, sir, ... it's difficult to explain.'

Cutler's face was two inches away. 'You bet your life it is!'

The Doctor stepped forward: 'I can assure you we mean you no harm, my dear General.'

'You can assure me what you like. Whether I'll believe you or not is another matter. You people land at a military installation without authorisation or even proper identification, in the middle of a complex space shot ...'

'A space shot!' exclaimed Polly excitedly.

Cutler took the cigar out of his mouth. 'I've no time to deal with this now.' He pointed the cigar almost threateningly at the three travellers. 'But by thunder, you'd better have a good explanation ready later.'

'I don't like your tone, sir,' the Doctor began.

A faint smile appeared on the General's craggy features.

'And I don't like your face, Grandad.'

Turning from the speechless Doctor, he beckoned to the Sergeant. 'Sergeant, bring them into the tracking room and keep them under guard in the observation chamber. I'll question them as soon as I have time.'

The sight of the Doctor and his two companions entering the space tracking room created a minor sensation. The technicians just stood and gaped—especially at the pretty girl with the long blonde hair, blue eyes, and tall, shapely figure. Barclay strode across to meet the General: 'What on earth ...?' he began.

'Never mind now,' said Cutler brusquely. He motioned the Sergeant to take the three time travellers into the observation chamber at the side of the main tracking room. As soon as the three had filed into the narrow room, the General turned around and motioned the men back to their places: 'O.K., let's get back with it, we've a job to do.'

Cutler strolled past the seated men like a school teacher with a class of unruly boys, eyeing them carefully before taking his usual place on the dais.

'What are they doing here, Doctor?' Polly whispered excitedly. 'Is it some kind of space shot?'

Ben nodded and turned to the Doctor. 'Yeah, a smaller version of Houston Space Control. Mind you, not quite what you see on TV, is it?'

The deep voice of the Sergeant, who had taken his place behind them in the viewing room, cut in: 'Don't know what you've seen on your TV, son, but this is General Cutler's outfit. He don't like a lot of personnel. Cuts them down to the bare minimum and works 'em into the ground. We only do a couple of months stretch on this station.'

The Doctor, who had been studying the wall behind them, suddenly cleared his throat with a little clicking noise he sometimes made to attract their attention.

'I don't want to depress you, but we ... er ... are not quite where you think we are.'

'What do you mean, Doctor?' asked Ben.

The Doctor pointed to the calendar.

'I don't see anything ...' began Polly—and then her voice died away as she caught sight of the date: 2000! The year was 2000!

'Oh, not again,' she moaned. 'I really thought we were on our way home this time.'

Ben glumly nodded his agreement. 'Still adrift! That explains why there are so few people. Computers do all the work now.' He turned round to look at the Sergeant. 'Have they reached Mars yet?'

The Sergeant, more relaxed now, leant back against the wall and grinned. 'I thought you watched TV, sailor?'

'You mean you *have* sent people to Mars?'

20

'An expedition came back five months ago.'

'Has this flight anything to do with it?' Polly asked, pointing towards the astronauts on the screen which they could clearly see through the glass front of the observation booth.

'No. Just the normal atmosphere testing probe. Purely routine. Nothing ever happens ...'

Suddenly, the attention of the three became engaged by a flurry of activity inside the tracking room. The men were craning towards the main console. Barclay was gabbling into the communication phone: 'An error? Where?'

The voice of Williams boomed out over the loudspeakers:

'Looks bad. We are now over South Island, New Zealand. We're reading a height of eleven hundred miles.'

'Eleven hundred! That's impossible!' He glanced sideways. 'Dyson, check what it should be, will you?'

Dyson checked one of the illuminated dials. 'It should be nine hundred and eighty.'

The Australian jumped up and, leaning across his smaller English colleague, tapped the computer read-out key.

Again, the figure of nine hundred and eighty miles appeared on the dial.

'Cripes!' exclaimed Barclay. 'You're right! Nine hundred and eighty miles. Out of position by over one hundred miles.'

He spoke into the mike again: 'Snowcap to Zeus Four. Do you read me?'

The voice of the astronaut, crackling with static, came through on the loudspeaker.

'Zeus Four to Snowcap. Strength eight. Over.'

'Take visual checks on Mars to establish position, please. Repeat back.'

21

On the screen, they watched the coloured astronaut nod his head in agreement: 'Will do. Out.'

In the space capsule, Colonel Williams turned to Schultz. 'Did you get that, Dan?'

Schultz nodded grimly. The easy, relaxed atmosphere inside the small capsule had disappeared. Both men now spoke with a quiet deliberation and a charged awareness of their predicament.

'Go ahead then,' said Williams.

Schultz swung a small telescope viewer into position. He looked at the vernier on the telescope support. Beside him, William consulted a small chart fixed to the back of the instruments.

'Should be about four, two, zero.'

Schultz checked the verniers again. 'Nope. It's four, three, two.'

For a moment, the other astronaut's composure broke. 'Ah, come on man, it can't be. Try again.'

'O.K.' He manipulated the small telescope again.

'And get a move on. We'll be back in the sunrise shortly.'

Schultz glanced out of the corner of his eye at the younger man. 'Take it easy, Glyn. We've time.'

For a moment Williams struggled with his feelings and then, leaning forward slightly to speak into the mike to Snowcap base, he became the impersonal, all-systems-go astronaut.

'Did you hear that conversation?'

Dyson's voice came through on the loudspeaker. 'Yes, Colonel. We're getting a Mars fix, too. We'll call back.'

'O.K.' Williams nodded and tried relaxing back into his seat. 'I guess it's just . . .' he began, turning his head to Schultz. But his eye suddenly caught something rigid and fixed in the older man's stance as he twisted round to look through the telescope.

'Glyn?'

'Yes?' Williams felt a sudden prickle of fear. A new, grim note had crept into the astronaut's voice. If there was one man in the whole space establishment who never allowed the slightest emotion to show, it was the veteran Schultz.

'Now take it easy, but ...'

'For Christ's sake what is it?' Williams flared.

The older man turned round, eyes wide, face tautened. 'That wasn't Mars I had ...'

'Is that all?' Williams forced himself to relax. 'Well that explains it, doesn't it? C'mon, try again.'

Without turning, the other man slowly shook his head. 'No, listen, Glyn—there's something else out there.'

'Something else? What?'

'Another planet.'

'Another ... That's crazy! How can there be?'

For answer, Dan Schultz swung the telescope over to Williams' side on its hinged arm.

The younger man grabbed it and studied the object Schultz indicated through the capsule window. After a long minute, he slowly pushed the telescope aside, and turned to the veteran astronaut. 'You're right, Dan. There is something there. I can't see it properly, but it reads as if it were in orbit between Mars and Venus.'

Schultz nodded. 'That's it. You know, somehow— I just can't put my finger on it—but it looks kinda familiar.'

Their conversation was interrupted by the harsh sunlight of space entering through the windows. They squinted and turned their eyes away from the bright light. 'Came the dawn!' Schultz frowned.

'Yeah,' Williams nodded. 'We've had any further observations for a bit.' He turned back to the mike. 'Hello *Snowcap*. Hello *Snowcap*. We are now in dawn. Over San Francisco. Can you get this object from where you are?'

'You are very faint. Put up the power output, please,' replied Barclay.

Williams leant forward and spoke almost directly into the mike. 'Can you get this object on your retina-scope?'

'Can do,' replied Barclay's voice.

Williams' eyes suddenly became fixed on another dial close to the mike. 'Hey, Dan, look at this, will ya? That's odd!'

'Yeah.' Schultz turned round and followed the line of Williams' pointing finger.

'Our fuel cells are showing a power loss. A pretty sharp drop.'

The two men looked at each other anxiously.

'What the hell's happening here?'

3

The New Planet

The tracking station room was buzzing with anxious conversation. Some of the men were glued to the TV screen; others feverishly monitored the signals sent back to Earth.

Barclay and Cutler abruptly left the dias and strode over to the operator of the base telescope.

'Have you got it yet?' questioned Barclay.

The technician shook his head.

The telescope screen was clearly visible to the Doctor, Ben and Polly from the observation room.

Cutler nudged the technician: 'Hurry it up, fella.'

Ben suddenly became aware that the Doctor was indulging in another favourite habit. His head was tilted back, his eagle eyes were staring at the television screen, his right hand was nervously stroking his cheek. It meant only one thing: the Doctor had an idea.

Snatching out a little notebook and pencil, the Doctor hastily scribbled something. He finished and turned to the Sergeant standing beside him:

'Sergeant, give this to your General, will you?'

'Me?' The Sergeant looked startled. 'If you think I'd interrupt him at this time—you're crazy!'

'It may be vital. If you'll take me to the General, I'm sure I'll be able to help him.'

Recognising the note of command in the Doctor's voice, the Sergeant nodded and led them out of the observation room, and across to General Cutler, who

25

was gazing at the television screen.

The round outline of the planet which had been picked up by the base telescope, although badly out of focus, was clearly visible.

Without taking his eyes off the screen, Cutler spoke through his clenched teeth, the cigar still sticking from the corner of his mouth:

'What is it?'

'The old guy would like a word with you, sir. Claims it's urgent.'

'O.K.' He beckoned the Doctor over. 'Make it fast.'

The Doctor stared at the white pulsating circle of light on the screen. 'I think I know what you're going to see.'

'Eh? How can you.' he snapped. The Doctor ripped a page out of his notebook.

'It's all down here.' He flourished the paper, but the General took no notice. Instead, Barclay took the paper from his hand. Suddenly, Dyson, who had been standing on the other side of the telescope, called out: 'Quick, we've got it!'

Several technicians scrambled over to look at the screen. The circular blob of light had cleared; its outlines were sharp; they could make out an object somewhat like a golf ball in size, with light and shaded areas.

'It's a planet all right,' said Dyson.

'How can it be?' Cutler cut in. 'Planets can't just appear from nowhere. Mars is the nearest planet and it's way beyond this one.'

'It must be on an oblique orbit,' Barclay seemed to be almost speaking to himself.

'And approaching quite fast.' Dyson turned to the Australian. 'Of course, that's what's drawing off the capsule!'

Barclay nodded grimly. 'That's it all right. *Zeus Four*

is out of orbit, and the new planet is influencing it.'

'That's about it.' Dyson nodded. 'It has to be.'

'We must get them down—quick.'

'An emergency splash down?' Cutler, who had felt at a loss during the preceeding conversation between the more knowledgeable scientists, warmed to the prospect of action.

'Yes.' Barclay moved back to his console, and flicked the mike switch. '*Snowcap* to *Zeus Four*, come in please. Do you read me?'

After the initial crackle of static from the speaker, Williams' voice came over faint but clear: 'Yes, we read you loud and clear now.'

'You are strength two only. Please speak up.'

'Our fuel cells show a power loss.'

'Power loss? How much?'

'The main banks are down approximately twenty per cent.'

Barclay now spoke loudly and deliberately into the mike. 'We are going to bring you down now.'

'We need co-ordinates to correct orbit.'

'Stand by.'

'What the hell's going on anyway?'

'I don't know,' replied Barclay. 'Let's get you down here and find out later. O.K.?'

'Suits us,' answered the voice from space.

The two astronauts in the capsule were sweating visibly from the strain. Barclay's voice came over the loudspeaker.

'Corrected co-ordinates are: zero, zero, four, eight two zero and eight two three ...'

Williams began punching up the information. Leaning forward again, he shouted into the mounted microphone: 'Right. Now correct. Out.' He turned

27

to his companion. 'Are you ready on altitude jets, Dan?'

Schultz twisted slightly and grasped two joystick controls. 'Ready.'

'Go.'

Schultz pressed the buttons on the top of the joysticks; a metallic hissing roar came from outside the capsule—but the long bar of sunlight across their chests failed to shift its position.

Williams studied the instruments. 'Again.'

Once more Schultz stabbed the controls. The two men heard the same hissing roar from outside the capsule as the retro jets fired. Then, abruptly, the long bar of sunlight flashed into their eyes, almost blinding them.

'Look!' exclaimed Schultz. Outside the windows, in the full glare of the sun, the blue and white earth seemed to be spinning round the capsule in a dizzying kaleidoscope of colour.

'We're tumbling!' shouted Schultz.

'Use the manual controls.'

For the first time in his career experience, Major Schultz seemed almost paralysed, unable to act. His hands shook uncontrollably as the capsule swung round and round, wildly tumbling through space.

Williams put his broad hand on the other man's shoulder and gripped it. 'Come on, man, get with it.'

With an effort, Schultz shook his head, and snapped out of his momentary shock. He gripped the two joysticks, and heaved hard on the controls. 'I can't. It's too much for me!'

Williams quickly freed himself from the retaining safety belt, leant over and, putting his hands beneath the other man's, added his greater strength to the effort. Gritting their teeth, they inched the controls back until, gradually, the lighthouse-like beam of the sun—which had all this time been revolving wildly across their faces—slowed down and finally stabilised.

Williams eased back into his seat, leaving Schultz holding the controls. Their faces were wet with sweat; their breath laboured almost to the limits of their endurance.

'What's going on?' Williams grunted, painfully forcing his lungs to draw in air. 'I feel absolutely clapped out.'

Schultz nodded, his face grey. 'Something's taking all the power out of my body. What the heck's the matter now?'

Cutler was in full command of the splash-down operation. He barked into the mike in front of him: 'Hello Hawaii. *Zeus Four* will splash down at 1445 your time. All helicopters to area six immediately.'

The loudspeaker bleeped. 'Check. Full deployment at 1400. Out.'

Dyson was also playing his part in the splash-down operation. 'Hello Rome computer base. Final descent path. Please compute and repeat.'

A voice with a foreign accent spoke in reply. 'All re-entry vectors are programmed. Read out at 1350.'

Barclay glanced around the large tracking room. Each of the men was now totally intent upon his part in the complex splash-down procedure. He pulled the mike closer, and spoke loudly. 'Hello *Zeus Four*. Your flight path is now correcting.'

Schultz's voice surfaced over the angry flood of static. 'The power loss is now increasing. Something has happened to our limbs. We can hardly move.'

Barclay glanced anxiously at the screen. The picture of the two men was now flecked with little dots of white—as though the picture had encountered bad

29

interference at some point in its transmission from space.

'You've been up there a fair time. It's probably just space fatigue.'

'No ... it's quite different. We had to operate the manual controls together. Neither of us could have done it alone.'

Barclay anxiously examined the screen before replying. Then he glanced down at the paper Dyson had just slid along the top of the console, and replied. 'We have your descent path now. Stand by.'

The astronauts in the capsule were growing weaker and weaker. Each movement seemed to require an immense effort.

Barclay's voice came over the loudspeaker. 'Re-entry will begin in position four six zero, and verto rockets to go at fourteen, forty five.'

Williams slowly raised his arm and weakly began operating the rows of switches in front of him.

'Dan,' he croaked, 'put that into the computer, will you?'

Schultz, wincing from the effort, stretched out his arm and started programming the computer control in front of him.

'One thing, man,' gasped Williams into the mike, 'you'll have to bring us in this time round. We can't hang on any longer.'

The two men held their breath as they waited for the reply. Then Barclay's voice came over: 'You must. We can't bring you down this orbit. You'll over-shoot!'

With a sense of impending doom, the two men looked at each other wearily. The grey-haired older man shook his head: 'We'll never make it, Glyn.'

The big negro astronaut seemed to pull himself together. 'Yes we will. Come on, Dan, we'd better check the re-entry controls. Ready?'

Schultz nodded passively.

'Retros one and three.'

Schultz looked up at the dials: 'Check.'

'Main 'chute cover?'

'Yeah. O.K.'

'Heat shield bolts?'

'Yep.' The routine of checking the instruments was one that Schultz could practically do blindfold—the familiar re-entry pattern.

Suddenly Williams looked at the instruments above his head and anxiously glanced back at him. 'Dan, what do you make our position?'

Schultz leant over. His face contorted painfully. 'We've swung out again!'

Williams heaved forward, and shouted into the mike: 'Emergency! Emergency! We have left flight path again. Give correction please, urgent.'

4

Mondas!

Barclay jumped up and slammed down the clipboard on which he had been making notes. 'It must be that flaming planet. Its gravity is affecting the capsule.'

'What do we do about it?' asked Dyson, who was standing beside him.

'What *can* we do?' Barclay began—and then realised that the eyes of most of the men in the room were on him. He pulled himself together. 'First of all we must give *Zeus Four* a new correction path. Will you do that?'

Dyson nodded. 'Right away.'

'Then we must get a better fix on this so-called planet and try to identify it.'

He looked across at Cutler, who was standing by the television screen, and noticed that the General had undone the buttons of his tunic—something Cutler only did in extreme emergencies.

'It's considerably clearer now,' commented Cutler.

Barclay nodded then, remembering something, strode quickly across the floor of the control room towards the observation room. He beckoned to the Doctor.

When the Doctor appeared, he spoke quickly. 'You say you know something about this new planet? Let's have it.'

The Doctor looked away thoughtfully for a moment, and tapped his fingers on his lapels. 'Well, I'm not absolutely sure. Perhaps if I can look at it again.'

Barclay turned round and shouted across to one of the technicians: 'Feed the retinascope picture to the observation monitor.'

One of the nearby technicians pressed a button and the picture of the two astronauts was replaced by an image of a planet the size of a football. Barclay and the Doctor moved forward to observe it more closely.

'What about setting these boys down, eh, Dr Barclay?' shouted Cutler angrily from behind them.

But the scientist had been caught by something in the appearance of the new planet. 'Yes, yes,' shouted the Doctor excitedly, his eyes shining with the stimulus of a new idea. 'It's just as I thought. Perhaps you would care to examine these land masses here.' He pointed to one side of the screen. Cutler, caught by the urgent tone of the Doctor's voice, also turned round to examine the screen.

'Land masses. I don't see any ... Oh yeh, I see what you mean!'

The image of the strange planet was now fairly clear on the larger screen. Much of it was covered in white cloud masses, but they could make out the outline of a long triangle with slighly curved edges.

'Does that remind you of anything?' asked the Doctor.

Cutler shrugged his shoulders. 'No, I don't reckon so.'

Unnoticed by the others, the Sergeant, followed by Polly and Ben, had come up behind the Doctor.

It was Ben who spoke. 'Hey, it looks familiar, don't it?'

'Yes!' Polly moved a bit closer to the screen. 'Ben, look. That bit, surely that's ... South America!'

'Yeah! And look—the other side. Doesn't that look like ... Africa!'

'There is a marked similarity,' said Barclay slowly.

'Nonsense!' exclaimed Cutler. 'How could it be?'

For answer, Barclay pointed to the top of the map. 'Look. Surely that's Arabia, India ...'

The General nodded reluctantly. 'Well, O.K. It must be some reflection of Earth.'

'No.' The scientist was thinking aloud. 'It can't be that. There's nothing to reflect on.'

Behind him, the Doctor, a slightly self-satisfied expression on his face, had drawn himself up to his full height. 'Now,' he said, 'my dear sir, I suggest you look at that piece of paper I gave you.'

'Paper? Oh yes!' Barclay fumbled in his pocket and brought it out. His eyes opened wide with amazement as he read it. 'You knew?'

The Doctor nodded a little smugly. 'Certainly.'

'What did he know?' rapped Cutler.

Barclay held out the paper to the General. 'He has correctly written down what we have just seen and ...' He looked at the Doctor in amazement. '... he did it before we saw it!'

Cutler looked down suspiciously at the piece of paper in his hand. 'Some kind of con trick, that's all.'

But Ben noticed that from now on he seemed to treat the Doctor with a wary respect.

Barclay shook his head. 'No, no, I remember when he gave me the bit of paper.' He turned back to the Doctor. 'You really know a great deal about this situation. Can you be more explicit?'

The Doctor nodded and grasped the lapels of his cloak. He looked a little like a school teacher addressing a class. 'Yes, I'm sorry to say that I can. Millions of years ago Earth had a twin planet called Mondas ...'

'Get lost! We've no time to listen to this ...' Cutler turned away in disgust and called to the technician manning the communications console. 'Get me

Geneva on the radio link.' He turned back to Barclay. 'We'll see what Secretary Wigner has to say about this.' He strode over to the communications console, Barclay following him.

Polly turned angrily to the Doctor. 'How can he be so rude to you? What's the matter, Doctor? You're looking terribly worried.'

'Really? Yes, I suppose you could say I'm a little worried.'

'Tell us then, Doctor. What's happening?' pleaded Ben.

'You see, Ben—I know what this planet is and what it means to Earth.'

'Means to Earth!' echoed Ben. 'How can it affect us?'

The Doctor gazed up at the ceiling. His companions noticed that his cheek was twitching in agitation. He spoke slowly and deliberately: 'Before very long, I'm afraid we must expect ... visitors!'

'Visitors? Out here at the South Pole? Come off it, Doctor! Who do you think's going to bring them? Santa Claus on his sledge?'

But the Doctor didn't appear to have heard Ben. He was watching Cutler, who was speaking into the console. 'Quiet boy, quiet.'

Cutler's loud voice echoed through the tracking room. 'Is that I.S.C. Geneva? Put me through to the Secretary-General. Yes, that's right.'

The Doctor turned to the Sergeant who was standing behind them. 'May I ask who that is?'

'Gee!' The Sergeant seemed genuinely surprised. 'You really are out of touch, aren't you? That's Secretary-General of International Space Command: Robert Wigner!'

Secretary Wigner, supreme commander of the International Space Command, was seated at his desk in the Geneva headquarters. A compact, dark-haired man of about forty, his round, slightly pudgy face gave no indication of his formidable character. He was respected throughout the world as an extremely efficient—even ruthless—administrator, with an enormous intelligence.

The large, circular crest of International Space Command—a globe with an outstreched hand holding a spaceship pointing towards the stars—dominated the wall behind him.

Wigner spoke into one of his many radio-phones. 'This is very hard to believe, General. Are you quite sure?'

Cutler's voice came through on the suspended loudspeaker system. 'There's no doubt at all.'

Wigner thought for a moment and then nodded. 'Very well. Just a moment please.' He turned to one of his aides.

'Get on to Mount Palomar and ask them to provide us with a picture as soon as possible.' He turned to another colleague. 'Contact Jodrell Bank and ask them to get an exact fix on this "planet". We must have data—and quickly!'

He turned back to the radio-phone. 'Let me know the moment you have any more information, General.'

Wigner leant back for a moment and looked across at a large wall map on which red circles marked the various space tracking stations. His grey eyes looked cold and thoughtful.

Cutler's voice came through again. 'One more thing, sir.'

Wigner, shaken out of his thoughts, leant forward impatiently. 'Yes?'

'We have three intruders.'

36

'Intruders? At the Pole? Where did they come from?'

'We haven't interrogated them yet—but one of them seems to know quite a bit about this new planet.'

'I don't understand. How can he possibly know?'

'We'll find out, Mr Secretary.'

'Do that immediately, relay at once any further information.'

In the tracking room, Cutler turned to face the Doctor and his companions.

'O.K. You heard the Secretary-General. Now suppose you tell me how you really got here.'

'Ah,' replied the Doctor, 'that will be rather difficult.'

'Not nearly as difficult as I can be. You'd better believe that, Doctor.' Cutler's powerful frame was looming over him, his large jaw jutting forward. 'Now listen. You turn up from nowhere. A routine space shot goes wrong. A new planet appears. You tell us you know all about it. That puts you in the hot seat. Right?'

The Doctor looked puzzled. 'Hot seat?'

'On the carpet,' Ben whispered.

'We've got nothing to do with it,' complained Polly quickly.

'Can you prove it?'

'Well,' began the Doctor a little nervously, 'if you let us return to where we came from, you would not be troubled further——' The Doctor turned—and met the hard gaze of the Sergeant who was standing behind him. His fingers were tapping the strap of his machine gun, which was still slung loosely over his shoulder.

'You're not going anywhere, Doctor,' replied the General. As though remembering something, he turned back to the Sergeant. 'Have you searched that hut of theirs·yet?'

'No, sir.'

'Why the devil not?' Cutler exploded. 'Send your men out there and get it done now—then we might get to the bottom of this!'

Outside, it was still snowing hard. Had the Sergeant and his men been out a moment sooner, they would have seen, dimly visible through the murk, a long black torpedo-like object coming into land just beyond the TARDIS ...

As it landed, it gave out a high-pitched winnowing sound and a red light mounted on top flashed briefly. Over the roar of wind there was a faint bubbling radiophonic noise from the body of the object. Then all noise ceased, and the long, rocket-like object began to disappear beneath the driving snow.

The trap door opened with a splintering crack of ice and one by one, the parka clad figures of the Sergeant, Tito and a third soldier emerged from the warmth of the Base. Tito was carrying a small portable electric drill powered by a set of back batteries, and the other soldier, a crowbar. They looked around them: nothing but snow everywhere ...

The Sergeant pointed in the direction of the TARDIS and, balancing themselves against the strong wind, they staggered across the snow towards it. They completely failed to see the long black object, which had nestled deep in the snow beyond the police box.

The three men ran their hands over the surface of the TARDIS. It seemed to be made of some sort of metal. The Sergeant tried to open the door, but found it locked. He banged it with his fist, heaved against it with his shoulder—but without success.

Tito now came forward with the drill, flicked the switch, and applied it to a point just above the lock. The Sergeant and the other men watched as a wisp of smoke began to rise from the drill point. Tito groaned and switched it off.

'What's up?' asked the Sergeant.

Tito held up the hand-drill: the end had fractured clean off. 'Dunno what the heck that metal is, Sarge, but it's too tough for this drill.'

The Sergeant nodded. 'Reckon we're going to need a welding torch to get inside this thing. Get back inside and bring me one out—and bring an extra helper. You'll need someone else to help.' Tito shambled off.

The crowbar proved equally useless.

The Sergeant began kicking the TARDIS in disgust, and beating his hands on his ribs to keep warm.

From behind the TARDIS, a strange radiophonic bubbling sound penetrated through the blizzard.

The two men stopped stamping and turned round. 'What's that! Hey, Tito, is that you?' The sound stopped.

The Sergeant looked at the other soldier, shrugged his shoulders and turned back to the TARDIS again. The soldier tapped him on the shoulder. 'Sarge.'

'Yeah,' mumbled the Sergeant, irritated. Every time he spoke he had to pull down his face mask, and he was acquiring a beard of white frost all around his mouth and nose. 'What is it?'

The man pointed beyond the TARDIS. The Sergeant looked. Three lights were moving towards them through the murk of the blizzard. Again the radiophonic bubbling sound, now slightly raised in pitch, drifted across the frozen waste.

'What's going on? Who the heck's that?' The Sergeant tried to rub the snow from the outside of his goggles to clear them—then realised that it was frozen condensation within. He whipped them off in disgust and, shielding his eyes, peered through the snow.

The three lights were slowly changing into three tall, straight figures which were moving forward across the ice with a slow, deliberate step, and the perfect unison of guardsmen on parade.

The Sergeant swung the gun from his shoulder, and challenged the three figures: 'O.K. Stay right there.'

But the tall figures, each one seemingly clad in a silver armoured suit, continued to move inexorably towards them.

'I warn you,' shouted the Sergeant, 'one more step and I'll open fire.'

The Sergeant gazed, horror-struck, as they came nearer and nearer. He made out their chests—which resembled concertina-like packs. For heads, they had helmets with side handles, a mounted light, circles for eyes and a slit for a mouth. Seen at closer quarters they were much more like robots than human beings!

Jerking up his machine gun, he aimed and pulled the trigger. The mouth of the gun spurted fire and a stream of bullets sprayed across the marching figures. To his horror the bullets seemed to have no affect whatsoever! Not for one moment did they stop their steady march towards the two frightened men.

Finally, the gun jammed in the bitter cold, and the Sergeant swung it back to club down the nearest figure—who was now directly in front of him. Before he could do so, the leading figure raised an arm and swung it downwards in a terrible chop.

With a cry, the Sergeant staggered backwards and collapsed in the snow. His sightless eyes gazed up; his head—the neck completely shattered—lolled at a grotesque angle.

The other soldier, meanwhile, had been backing

away, brandishing the crowbar in front of him like a quarterstaff. Suddenly, one of the robot figures reached forward and grasped the end of it.

After a brief tug-of-war, the robot, exerting his tremendous strength, swung his arm up, and lifted the man right off his feet, holding him suspended at arm's length. Quickly the soldier let go, but before he could scramble to his feet, the robot had swung the heavy bar effortlessly through the air and had brought it crashing down on the soldier's head, smashing helmet and skull like an eggshell. The man lay motionless in death; a red stain began to taint the snow.

Two minutes later, Tito and another soldier emerged from the trap door with the welding equipment.

Peering through the driving snow, they glimpsed two parka-clad figures standing by the TARDIS. Tito called out to them: 'Hey, Sarge, this should do it, eh?' Neither figure turned.

'Sarge——' Tito's voice choked in his throat as the parka-clad figures by the TARDIS turned round, their hoods falling away to reveal the blank masks of Cybermen.

The soldiers, loaded down with the heavy welding equipment, didn't stand a chance. The two giant figures moved forward and dealt two more deadly blows.

For a moment, the leading Cyberman looked down at the two crumpled figures. He then gestured to one of his companion robots, who knelt down and began to divest the two dead men of their parka jackets and thick leggings ...

5

The Cyberman Invasion

Inside the tracking room, General Cutler, cigar held loosely between his lips, feet on the console in front of him, was leaning back in his chair. The Doctor, who was standing beside him, had just finished telling his story.

'That's the most fantastic story I've ever heard. You can't expect us to believe that, Doctor.'

The Doctor looked a trifle huffy. 'I can only repeat what I have already said. We must expect visitors from that planet.'

Cutler shook his head. 'Not a chance. Anyway, we've more important things to think about right now.' He turned to Barclay. 'What's the position in the capsule, Tom?'

'They have full instructions, General. I'm just doing the final check.'

Cutler swung his legs off the desk and walked across to the radar technician. 'What's the range?'

'One thousand two hundred and fifty miles, sir.'

'How far are they off course?'

'Two hundred and thirty miles.'

'Then it's increasing.'

'Yes, I'm afraid it is, sir.'

Cutler walked back to the console, leant over the desk, and spoke into the mike. 'Attention *Zeus Four*. *Snowcap* here. Don't worry, boys—everything's under control. We'll get you down double quick. You'll be having supper in Hawaii tonight with all those lovely girls!'

'Get me Polar Base,' snapped Wigner,

Tension was mounting at the International Space Centre. The communications console at the far end of the room—formerly empty—was now manned by I.S.C. technicians. One of them turned to the Secretary General. 'We're having trouble there, sir.'

'Well keep trying.' Wigner turned in his chair, drummed his fingers on the desk, then leant forward and switched on the television monitor set in front of him. An announcer, familiar to millions of American homes, was standing beside a large globe of the Earth.

'Since it was first discovered at South Pole Rocket Base,' the commentator was saying, 'reports have been coming in from observatories over the world confirming its existence.' A piece of paper was slipped to him, which he seized, and then announced triumphantly, 'Here, straight from Mount Paloma Observatory is the first picture of our neighbour in space.'

As Wigner watched, the camera moved in for a close-up of the new 'Tenth Planet'—as the news media were already calling it.

'Some observers have reported that its land masses resemble those of Earth,' the commentator continued, 'but this is being hotly disputed in top astronomical circles, and no general agreement has yet been reached. Jodrell Bank, England, say that the planet is approaching Earth—but there is absolutely no cause for alarm. It won't come near enough to collide. I repeat—there is no danger.'

Wigner leant forward and switched off the monitor. He turned impatiently to the communications technician. 'What about Polar Base? Are you through?'

'No, sir, we can't get them.'

'What's happened?'

'There's some degree of interference.'

'What do you mean—interference? Who on earth would try to jam communications at a time like this?

The technician shook his head. 'I don't know, sir. It doesn't resemble any of the classic jamming techniques used by ...' he hesitated for a moment, '... other power blocks. This is something quite different. It's enormously powerful and—it seems to be coming from the *Snowcap* base itself!'

'May I have everyone's attention, please,' Barclay was standing by his console. He waited until all the men in the room were attending fully, and then continued, 'This is important—so please listen carefully. Final orbit beginning from base reference one is ...' he paused to look down at his console. '... four minutes ten seconds. Now we have an extremely difficult job on our hands. Everyone must be on their toes all the time. If the capsule power falls too low I shall take over re-entry from here, and for that I shall need all the radar tracking team behind me. Reference one commencing now.'

Inside the observation room, the three time travellers were sharing the general tension outside. 'They must bring them down right away,' remarked the Doctor.

'Why?' asked Polly.

'Because they will be quite unable to complete another orbit.'

'Hadn't you better tell them?' Ben motioned to the three men on the dais.

'They probably know already.'

Ben rose from the bench. 'Well, if you don't, I will.' He turned to leave the observation room—but the Doctor caught his arm and held it in an iron grip. Ben

44

winced. But the Doctor didn't seem to be aware of the pressure he was applying—something at the far end of the tracking room had caught his attention.

Three parka-clad figures had noiselessly entered, moved to the centre of the tracking room, and now stood immobile, their backs to the wall. Most of the occupants of the tracking room had their backs to them—and parka-clad soldiers were, anyway, a familiar enough sight. All Ben could see through the glass of the observation were three tall figures with their heads slightly bent—and a glimpse of snow goggles.

'What is it?' asked Ben.

'Stay—in—here.' The Doctor spoke urgently, and shook Ben's arm to punctuate his words.

'I don't get it. It's only those soldiers ...'

'No—look,' cried Polly. She let out a slight scream and held her hand to her mouth.

From the other side of the room, the three Cybermen were slowly removing their goggles. The time travellers could now see quite clearly the flat, expressionless masks, and the reflected glints of light as their hoods were thrown back to reveal the menacing silver helmets.

Suddenly, a nearby technician turned—his mouth fell open, thunderstruck. He was followed by others. One by one the men became aware and turned to face the new arrivals.

Cutler, sitting on the dais with his back to them, was the last to notice. He caught sight of the men rising from their consoles and backing away from the three visitors.

'What the devil!' he called. 'Get back to your places.' Then he turned and saw the tall, menacing figures.

A soldier standing guard at the other end of the

45

room saw the Cybermen, reached for his carbine, and took aim. The nearby technicians ducked under their consoles. In response, one of the Cybermen casually raised a short silver baton-like object, and levelled it.

The soldier's shot rang out across the room. It was followed almost immediately by a red flash and a short hard noise like a football rattle from the Cyberman's weapon. The soldier froze in his tracks, the carbine dropped from his hands, and he fell back against the console. Smoke spiralled upwards from the openings in his uniform.

'Oh no!' Polly moved past the Doctor to go to the aid of the fallen soldier, but was stopped by Ben.

'Stay where you are, Duchess. They'll blow your head off.' He pulled her back inside the observation room.

Everyone was waiting breathlessly for the Cybermen's next move. Finally, Cutler flung his cigar on the floor, stamped on it and stood up. 'Everyone back to their places.'

The Cyberleader Krail, who had fired on the soldier, stepped forward. His flat, monotonous voice spoke sharply. 'Stop.'

Cutler, his face black with rage, turned on the Cyberman. 'I don't know what you are, or who you are, but we've got two men up in space and if we don't act now they won't get down alive.'

The Cyberman replied in the same flat, inexpressive monotone. 'They will not return.'

There was a chorus of exclamations from the men in the room.

'Not return?' spoke up Barclay. 'Why not?'

The Cyberleader waited until the chorus of voices had died down.

'It is unimportant.'

'Like hell!' Cutler flared. 'We must get them down.

46

Get out of my way.' He started to move towards the radar screen—but was blocked by the Cyberman.

'There is no point,' the Cyberleader continued. 'They could never reach Earth now.'

The three time travellers came out of the observation room. Polly walked up to the Cyberleader.

'But don't you care?'

'Care?' the Cyberleader repeated. 'I do not understand.'

'Care because they're people. They're going to die.'

'There are people dying all over your world. Do you "care" for all of them?'

'But ...' Polly floundered, 'we might save these two men.'

The Cyberleader ignored her and strode slowly and ponderously towards the head dais. He addressed Barclay. 'You will be wondering what has happened. Your astronomers must have just discovered a new planet. Is that not so?'

Barclay nodded excitedly. 'Yes, that's right.'

'That is where we come from. It is called Mondas.'

'Mondas,' Barclay repeated. 'Isn't that one of the ancient names for Earth?'

'Yes. Aeons ago the planets were twins. Then we drifted away from you to the very edge of space. Now we have returned.'

Ben turned to the Doctor and spoke under his breath. 'You were right, Doctor.'

General Cutler, confused by this exchange, strode forward and tried to reassert his authority.

'But who, or ...' He looked at their shining, silver-clad limbs—obviously made from a plastic-and-metal alloy. '... *what* are you?'

'We are called Cybermen,' replied the Cyberleader. 'We were exactly like you once. Then our Cybernetic scientists realised that our race was weakening.'

'Weakening? How?' asked Barclay.

'Our life span was contracting, so our scientists and doctors invented spare parts for our bodies until we could be almost completely replaced.'

'But,' Polly burst in, 'that means you're not like us. You're not people at all, you're ... robots!'

'That is not so. Our brains are just like yours except that certain ... weaknesses have been removed.'

'Weaknesses?' repeated Barclay. 'What weaknesses?'

Behind him, Cutler started edging back towards his console.

'You call them emotions, do you not?'

'But that's terrible!' exclaimed Polly. 'You mean you wouldn't feel for someone in pain?'

'There would be no need. We do not feel pain.'

'But we do.' Polly's eyes flashed. Alone of all the people in the room, she seemed completely unafraid of the three tall visitors from space.

Shielded by Barclay and the other men, Cutler reached the console. He lunged forward and pressed down the call switch to the International Space Command headquarters.

Krail's two assistants immediately raised their guns to fire at him—but the Cyberleader raised a restraining hand and walked over to the General.

Cutler stared at him defiantly. 'That'll stop you. I've just declared a state of international emergency!'

Wigner was speaking urgently to his conference colleagues at International Space Command.

'It seems to me that there is a pattern. Number one —a new planet appears. Number two—the Earth is losing its energy. Number three—the planet gets nearer and the energy loss increases. This, to my mind, connects the two. Exactly how, I don't know.

But ... yes, what is it?'

One of the technicians by the communications console had stood up to catch his attention. 'An emergency buzz from the Pole, sir.'

'What do they say?'

'Nothing, sir. It went off again immediately.'

Wigner looked around at the other men and pondered for a moment. 'Heavy static, emergency signal—they're in serious trouble, sir.'

He nodded to the waiting technician. 'Get them on the emergency microwave link.'

The tension in the space tracking room had reached fever pitch. Only the Cybermen themselves seemed to show no signs of having been affected by the situation. The Cyberleader, his voice flat and monotonous as ever, began to speak to Cutler. 'You will——'

A loud, intermittent buzzing interrupted him. A red light started flashing behind the dais. Cutler smiled triumphantly at the Cyberleader.

'Now,' continued the Cyberleader, 'you will pick up the radio and tell Europe International Space Command that nothing further has happened and that all is well here.'

Cutler shook his head firmly. 'No way!'

'That is an order.' The Cyberman's flat electronic voice only emphasised the menace in his words.

'I refuse—and there's nothing you can do about it.' The tall General's head was almost on a level with that of the Cyberleader. He stared hard at the blank circular eye holes as if trying to probe through to the mind within.

For a moment, the Cyberman seemed to pause indecisively.

'They're going to back down,' whispered Polly in

49

excitement. But Ben quickly put his hand over her mouth before the Cyberman could catch another word.

The Cyberleader put his hand to his chest unit and turned one of the knobs mounted on its concertina-like surface. A blinding flash of light—similar to a photographic flash gun—streaked out from the mounted light on the Cyberman's helmet. It seemed to stretch in a long vivid blue arc to the side of General Cutler's head. He screamed with pain, his head jerked back, and he crumpled to the floor.

As the man nearest to him rushed forward to help, Krail gestured to him to stay back.

'You murderers!' Polly shouted. 'You've killed him!'

6

Ben into Action

At the order of the Cyberleader, one of the Cybermen bent down, lifted the heavy body of the American General as easily as that of a five-year-old child, and stretched him out along the top of the nearest console. Apart from a slight black burn mark where the lightning flash had struck, the General seemed to be unharmed.

'He is not dead,' confirmed the Cyberleader. 'He will recover.'

There was a gasp of relief from the assembled men.

'Now,' continued the Cyberleader, looking around, 'who will give the message to your space commander?' His eyes came to rest on Dyson, and a long silver arm pointed towards him. Dyson fell back, face sweating, mouth sagging open with fear.

'You—which are the communication controls?'

Dyson quickly turned and walked over to the R/T communication console.

'Dyson,' Barclay's voice was like a whip lash. 'Think what you're doing, man!'

The Englishman turned to face him. His face was twisted with agony and fear. 'What else can we do? They'll kill us all.'

For a moment Barclay hovered uncertainly and then turned to the Cyberleader. 'What are you going to do?'

'You will see,' replied Krail.

The Cyberleader reached down and unclipped the

long Cyberweapon that had killed the guard. He brought it up and took aim at the centre of the communications console.

'No!' cried Barclay. He rushed forward and interposed his body between the Cyberleader's gun and the R/T set. 'If you destroy those, all contact with the space capsule will be broken!'

Dyson turned to Barclay. 'For God's sake, man, do as he asks. His voice quavered. 'Do you want the place destroyed?'

The tall Australian hesitated for a moment—and then nodded. 'All right.' He picked up the desk microphone.

'Hello, Geneva. Hello, Geneva.'

After a brief crackle of static, the waiting men heard the voice of Wigner over the R/T loudspeaker.

'*Snowcap*—at last! What's going on? We received an emergency call from you on the micro-link.'

Barclay wiped his brow for a moment. 'Ah, yes—it was—an error, sir. We're working on it now. Sorry about the false alarm.'

'Where is this static coming from? We can hardly hear you—even on this band.'

Barclay looked round, desperately searching for an explanation. The Cyberleader, standing right in front of him, slowly raised the gun until it was on a level with his face.

'I—I—er—it's most likely to have been the reactor. We had the moderator rods out for a short while this afternoon.'

After a long pause, Wigner spoke again. 'I see. Contact us if you have any further reports on this new planet.'

'Yes, sir.' Barclay leant forward and switched off the R/T set with his trembling hand. Without looking further at the Cybermen and the other men, he staggered back to his console and collapsed into his seat. Dyson followed him over and put his hand on his shoulder.

'We'd have all done exactly the same, Dr Barclay. We had no option.'

Barclay looked up, pushed Dyson's hand off his shoulder and, with sudden resolve, stood up and walked across to the Cyberleader. His voice rang round the tracking room.

'Right. We've done what you asked. Now you must let us try to recover our astronauts.'

'I told you—it is impossible for them to get back now. The pull of Mondas is too strong.'

'You can at least let us try!'

'It is a foregone conclusion—you are wasting your time. However, if you wish to contact them, I have no objection.'

Krail turned to the other two Cybermen.

'He and his colleagues may use their equipment. Any attempt at deceit—kill them at once.' The Cyberleader pointed to the body of the dead soldier. 'Take that out of here.'

As the Cybermen dragged the body of the soldier from the room, Barclay desperately tried to make contact with the two stranded astronauts.

'*Zeus Four, Zeus Four*, come in please. *Zeus Four, Zeus Four*, come in.'

After what seemed an age, the voice of Colonel Williams came through.

'We have you. Over.'

'Prepare to check orbital vectors.'

Meanwhile, Ben had been edging closer to the Doctor. He now leant across and spoke in his ear.

'While they fight it out, Doctor, let's make a break for it.'

'Eh? Break for it?'

53

'Yes. We can get back to the TARDIS.'

'How, my boy?'

'We can run for it—down that corridor to the trap door, and bolt it behind us.'

The Doctor shook his head. 'They'd burn it down in a flash.'

Ben looked round desperately. 'There must be something we can do.' He spotted one of the carbines which had been dropped by the guard, and now stood propped against the wall. 'For a start, we can use that.'

Polly pricked up her ears. 'Ben, don't be crazy. They'll see you.'

Ben shook his head. He started edging his way across the room towards the gun ...

'Ground range computer.' All the men in the room were fully concentrating on the job in hand. They were relieved to be handling a familiar routine.

Williams' voice came over the loudspeaker. 'On target.'

'Steering jet fuel reserve?' queried Barclay.

Schultz's voice answered. 'Adequate.'

Ben had almost reached the gun. He glanced around quickly. The three Cybermen were looking fixedly, immobile as statues, towards Barclay and the wavering television picture of Schultz and Williams.

'Suit temperature,' continued Barclay.

With a quick motion, Ben bent down, grabbed the barrel of the carbine, and swung it behind him. Quick as his action had been, it had not escaped the attention of the Cyberleader. He wheeled round and advanced on the three time travellers.

For a moment Ben considered swinging the gun round, and letting fly—but Polly and the Doctor, who were standing beside him, might get hurt in the fight. He decided to wait for another opening.

The Cyberleader, looking taller and even more

54

terrifying at close range, halted in front of him.

'You do not seem to take us seriously.' He held out his hand. 'Give me that gun.'

Ben hesitated for a moment but, with the huge bulk of the Cyberman looming over him, he had no option. He meekly brought the gun round and handed it over. The Cyberman gazed at it for a second and, without any apparent effort, flexed both his arms.

The Doctor's companions watched in horrified amazement as he splintered and broke away the wooden stock, bending the barrel—as easily as if it had been wire—into a right angle.

'When will you humans learn? Your weapons are useless against us!' The Cyberman flung the gun aside, then turned to the remaining Cybermen. 'Take him away.'

'Oh no!' Polly screamed, holding on to Ben's arm. But Ben shook her off. 'If he wanted to kill me, Duchess, he'd do so—just like that.'

'Yes.' The Cyberleader echoed his words. 'It is quite useless to resist us. We are stronger and more efficient than you earth people. We must be obeyed.'

Polly and the Doctor watched as the Cyberman lead Ben from the room.

7

Battle in the Projection Room

The Cyberman, holding Ben's wrists in a vice-like grip, half pulled and half dragged him along the corridors.

The Cyberman halted at a door at the end of the corridor. He checked that its lock contained a key, turned it, and flung the door open. With a swing of his arm, he threw Ben into the room, and slammed the door shut.

Rubbing his wrists, which were bruised and numb from the crushing grip of the silver giant, Ben rose from the floor and tried the door handle. Locked.

He flung his shoulder against it—and added another bruise to his collection. Rubbing his shoulder, he looked around curiously. Where had they put him?

One glance identified his location. When he had been flung through the door, he had collided with a film projector mounted on a tall metal stand. To its left stood a bench; above it, a rack of film cans.

The camera projected through a glass panel at the end of the room. Ben rushed eagerly over and peered through—but the base cinema beyond was in darkness. There was no other way out.

The two astronauts, now haggard and sweating, strained to hear Barclay's voice through the heavy static. The beam of light from the windows now swung slowly across their chests. It had almost stabilised.

'You begin exactly eighty seconds from now. Are you ready to go?'

Williams glanced across at Schultz, who nodded.

'Yes, we're ready.' Williams spoke as loudly, and with as much strength as he could muster into the microphone.

'Our readings show that you need forward correction of seven degrees.'

Williams glanced down at an instrument. 'That checks. We will correct with altitude controls.' He nodded to Schultz: 'Go ahead, Dan.'

Schultz reached for the joystick controls, forcing his muscles to work with a great effort. He manoeuvred the controls carefully, checking the instrument panels as he did so. Then he pressed the retro-rocket switch for a brief second.

Both men heard with relief the hissing roar of the rocket motors from outside the capsule. Schultz leaned forward excitedly, examined the dial reading, and gave the thumbs up sign to Williams.

'Hello, *Snowcap*,' Schultz cried. 'We have re-orientated the capsule. Altitude now correct.'

Barclay's voice rasped over the loudspeaker. 'Retro rockets to go in twenty seconds. After I give you the word, you come in on your own. Right?'

Williams nodded. 'Will do.'

The decision had not been an easy one. It meant that the two astronauts would have to fly their capsule manually without any help from the base computer. The important thing now was to slow the capsule down from its orbiting speed to re-entry velocity. A slow enough speed to enable them to land safely, drawn down by the Earth's gravity.

But was there enough power to 'brake' the capsule? Again, Schultz's hand moved towards the switch labelled RETRO.

Barclay was counting down. 'Seven, six, five, four, three, two, one—fire!'

Schultz pressed the switch. There was an immediate low-pitched thundering as the powerful retro rockets fired.

The two astronauts were slammed back in their seats, their faces flattening in the characteristic stretching of a person subject to heavy negative G-forces. The whole capsule was being vibrated. The teeth of the two astronauts were chattering from the heavy shaking.

The roaring went on for seven long seconds, then, abruptly, shut off. The faces of the two men contracted back to normal and they shook their heads in relief.

'Check the velocity, Dan,' Williams said. 'I'll do the ground check.'

Schultz nodded, rubbed his brow slightly as if to clear his vision, and peered forward at the instruments. His expression suddenly changed as he read the speed indicator dials. 'We're not down to re-entry velocity!'

'What!' Williams leant over to check Schultz's reading.

'No doubt about it. We're still at fourteen five. We should be down to eleven two!'

'Quick,' said Williams. 'We'll have to use the retros again.'

'Right.' Schultz reached for the switch, studying the instruments. He glanced over at Williams. 'How long for, Glyn?'

Williams, who was manipulating one of the small on-board computers, pointed his finger as the answer clicked up on a dial: '4.2 seconds.'

Schultz adjusted a control in front of him.

'Are you ready?' asked Williams.

They both braced themselves in their seats, their faces tense and set.

'Fire!'

Again, the capsule began to vibrate violently beneath their feet; the thunderous noise was almost deafening, their faces contorted with the pressure. This time it lasted for 4.2 seconds. Once again the two men relaxed back, shook themselves, and waited for the blood to return to their heads. Every movement now caused them acute pain; both felt weak and exhausted.

'What's it now?'

Schultz was peering at the instrument panel.

'Hurry up!' shouted Williams impatiently. Then he saw that the older man looked stricken, almost paralysed, with fright.

'It's fifteen one! We're not slowing ... we're speeding up ... uncontrollably!'

Williams leant back incredulously, rubbing the sweat from his brow. 'O.K. Fire the retros again!'

Exerting almost superhuman effort, Schultz managed to stretch his trembling fingers to make contact with the operating switch.

Once more, the hissing roar of the rocket motors shook the space capsule. This time it cut off abruptly after only two seconds.

Schultz looked at the fuel gauge, his face white with fear. 'The fuel's completely out—gone!'

Williams leant forward, shouting into the mike: 'Emergency! Emergency! Calling *Snowcap*. Emergency!'

In spite of the heating, every limb in Polly's body was trembling—she might just as well have been outside in the snow! Half the personnel of the base were clustered around the monitor, their eyes anxiously riveted to the drama of the stranded astronauts.

Behind them, impassive as statues, stood the Cybermen.

'Look at that damn radar now,' exclaimed Dyson. 'They're accelerating!'

Polly shuddered and wrung her hands. 'Can't you do anything to help them?'

'Their retro fuel's gone,' Barclay answered.

'I don't understand!' Polly was looking desperately from one man to the other.

Before Barclay could answer, Dyson cut in. 'Their course is changing—yes. They're veering out now— accelerating at an enormous speed.'

The television picture of the two men inside the capsule, although streaked with 'snow', was still clearly visible on the fixed screen. The two men had donned their space helmets. As the time travellers watched horrified, they saw the cabin start to fill with smoke.

The two beams of light from the windows were gyrating wildly, the capsule was speeding faster and faster away from the Earth!

The astronauts were making grasping movements towards the joystick controls but, with the great energy loss and the G-forces produced by the intense acceleration, seemed completely unable to reach them.

'They're beyond escape velocity now,' said Dyson. 'They can't ...'

There was a sudden rise in the intensity of the light from the telescope screen—as though an invisible hand had turned up the brilliance control. The interior of the capsule cabin whitened; Polly, and the others had to shield their eyes from the bright glare of the screen. Then it slowly faded away until the television monitor went blank.

Polly took her hands from her eyes, and looked around uncomprehendingly. Dyson's head was bowed at the console; Barclay was holding on to the side of the desk, as though near to collapse.

One of the radar technicians leant over and flicked a switch, cutting off the almost unbearable screech of static from the loudspeakers.

In the sudden silence, Polly found her voice. 'What happened?'

'I'm afraid the capsule exploded, my dear,' replied the Doctor.

'You mean,' Polly stared helplessly at the screen, 'they're dead ... just like that?'

The Doctor put his arm round her shoulders and, at the same time, looked over at the Cybermen. As if in answer to the Doctor's glance, Cyberleader Krail stepped forward.

'Now perhaps you can see that your planet is in great and imminent danger. In order to save you, we shall require information to be transmitted to Mondas.'

'Save us?' queried the Doctor.

'What about those poor men?' cried Polly.

'Now you will realise that you must co-operate with us. Mondas drew the ship away with its gravity. It was unavoidable.'

Dyson stood up. 'How? What's happening?'

The Cyberleader turned to him. 'The energy of Mondas is nearly exhausted. It now returns to its twin planet for energy.'

'It will take the energy away from Earth?' queried the Doctor.

'For how long?' Barclay broke in.

'Until it is completely exhausted,' replied the icy, monotonous voice of Krail.

'But that means that nothing will work—light,

61

power, engines, planes, ships!' exclaimed Dyson. 'The Earth will die!'

'Yes, everything on Earth will stop.'

Barclay strode forward. 'This is monstrous! You calmly tell us we're all going to die?'

'*You* are not.'

'Then how do you propose to stop the energy drain to Mondas?' asked the Doctor.

'We cannot. It is beyond our powers.'

'Then how can we expect to survive?' said the Doctor.

'By coming with us.' The Cyberleader now had the full attention of every man in the room. 'We are going to take you all back to Mondas.'

Ben had been hunting around the Projection Room in search of a weapon. Suddenly, his eyes fell upon a long screwdriver. He looked at it for a moment, balanced it in his hand—then drove it into the table. It fell out on to the floor—too blunt to stick in.

'Imagine trying to tackle one of them geezers with a screwdriver!' Ben said to himself, in disgust.

He leant back against the projection table—then nearly fell to the floor as it moved backwards on its trolley wheels. He turned round to examine it.

'Here! Half a mo'!' An idea began to dawn. 'If I turn it on that door, the Cybermen won't be able to see!'

Ben studied the projection table for a moment, then looked at the projector itself. A reel of film was ready loaded. After a moment the sailor found the right switch and pressed it.

The film began to move through the projector gate; a flickering image appeared on the wall by the projection window. Ben recognised it immediately:

Roger Moore as *James Bond*.

'Cripes! I saw that film just a few weeks ago!' He shook his head and thought again. 'Twenty years or so by their time!'

He glanced back at the film rack. Round the side of each of the reels, the title of the film had been written in large black letters on white tape.

'Ain't there nothing more recent than this?' But the other titles were unfamiliar to him. He piled the film cans on the edge of the bench, then turned to the projection table and swung it in a big arc. The coloured image of the film flittered over the bench and piled up films, ending on the white surface of the door.

Ben walked over and switched off the light. In the darkness, the square image of the film was clearly visible. Bond was fighting a gang of black-clad Karate students!

He watched it for a moment, then shrugged. 'Easy aint it, Commander! Like to see how you'd handle a Cyberman!' He smiled to himself. 'Wouldn't mind having you in here—just the same!' Picking up the screwdriver, he walked to the door, and started banging on it with the metal grip. Silence.

'Hey, Silver!' Ben shouted. 'Where are you?'

He continued banging with the screwdriver. Surely the noise would carry to almost every part of the base?

Finally, Ben watched as the key began to turn in the lock. He shuddered with fear—too late to be scared now! Ben stood behind the door, waiting. Only the flickering beam of the projector illuminated the near-dark room.

Clang! The Cyberman flung the door back and stepped in. For a moment, the silver giant, caught in the glare from the projector beam, was blinded. Only for a split second—but it gave Ben his chance! He flung the screwdriver at the cans of film. They collapsed with a deafening clatter. As the Cyberman wheeled round, Ben snatched the Cyberweapon from its retaining clips on the Cyberman's thigh.

Leaping to avoid a deadly chop, Ben aimed the weapon at the Cyberman's chest. The edge of the Cyberman's hand caught the door, slamming it shut with a metallic clang.

The Cyberman pressed a button on his chest unit. A dazzling beam of light from the Cyberman's helmet illuminated Ben, who was crouching behind the door.

'Do not resist, give me that weapon.'

Ben shook his head. 'Sorry, mate, I'm giving the orders now.'

The Cyberman paused for a moment, looked at the weapon held in Ben's hand, then started to move towards him.

As the Cyberman's arm slashed round in another terrible chop, Ben ducked and scurried behind the projector table. The Cyberman's hand shattered the bench and sent the remaining cans tumbling to the floor. They burst open, spilling out great loops of film.

'Look! I'm warning yer,' screamed Ben. 'I'll fire!'

The Cyberman moved forward inexorably, sweeping the projection table back against the wall with one flick of his arm. Ben looked around desperately. The tangled reels of film were blocking his escape route. He was trapped. The Cyberman raised his arm to deliver the death blow.

Ben closed his eyes, pointed the Cyberweapon at the Cyberman's chest unit, and pressed the button.

There was a loud, hard rattle. The Cyberman staggered back. The light abruptly went out on his helmet and smoke started curling from his neck and from the armour-like cracks between his arms and

64

shoulder units. As Ben watched, horrified, the giant's body stiffened and crashed backwards to the floor.

After several tense seconds of waiting, Ben plucked up courage to walk over to the dead Cyberman. Still aiming the Cyberweapon, Ben poked him gingerly with his toe.

There was no sign of life. The Cyberman's plastic chest unit had melted—as though from a terrible heat. A wisp of smoke was still rising from the blackened edges of a jagged, circular hole ...

Ben shook his head ruefully. 'You didn't give me no alternative, did you?'

Stepping over the body, he cautiously opened the door of the Projection Room ...

8

Two Hundred and Fifty Spaceships

The Cyberleader had listened sternly to the protests of the assembled base scientists. Now he raised a hand for silence.

'We will not argue. You must either come with us, or fade away on a dying planet.'

Barclay shook his head. 'There is no scientific proof that this *is* a dying planet.'

'Anyway,' added Dyson, 'perhaps we'd prefer to take our chances here!'

'That is not possible,' replied the Cyberleader. 'You must come and live with us.'

'How can we live with you?' exploded Polly. 'You're so different. You have no feelings.'

'Feelings?' asked the Cyberleader. 'I do not understand ... feelings?'

'Emotions. Love, pride, hate ... fear.'

'Come to Mondas and you will have no need of feelings. You will become like us.'

Polly backed away, her eyes widening. 'Like you!'

The Cyberleader pointed to his chest unit. 'Here we have freedom from disease, protection against heat and cold, and true mastery of the elements. Do you prefer to die in misery?'

'Surely the Earth may not lose all its energy?' asked Polly.

'It is inevitable.'

'Then you don't mind if we all die?'

'Mind? Why should we mind?'

General Cutler, who was still lying stretched out on the console where the Cyberman had laid him, was slowly recovering consciousness. Grasping the situation immediately, he listened, eyes closed.

'Millions and millions of people are going to suffer and die,' continued Polly. 'Just because of you!'

Cutler cautiously opened his eyes. With his head turned to one side, he was in full view of the door leading to the corridor. As he watched, it opened— unnoticed by the two Cybermen who had their backs to it. To the General's surprise, Ben came crawling through on all fours, and closed the door noiselessly behind him. In his right hand, he held the Cyberweapon.

Ben quickly scuttled in his stockinged feet to the back of the console on which Cutler was lying.

At the other end of the tracking room, Polly was still confronting the Cyberleader.

'Don't you ever think of anything or anyone except yourselves?'

'We are equipped to *survive*. We are only interested in survival.'

'Give me that thing.' Cutler spoke in a whisper, but his voice, sounding close to Ben's ear, made the sailor start. He looked up quickly at the apparently unconscious man.

'You heard me, boy,' the General whispered fiercely. 'Pass me that weapon.'

Ben paused for a moment, then placed the Cyberweapon in the General's dangling hand. With iron self-control, Cutler kept the rest of his body apparently relaxed. No one else could have detected that he was now fully awake and alert.

'Your deaths would not affect us,' continued the Cyberleader. 'You are of no importance.'

'When you rebuilt your bodies,' blazed Polly, 'you

67 .

obviously forgot to include a heart!'

'That is one of your weaknesses we can do without.'

In one deft movement, General Cutler swung his legs over the side of the console, levelled the Cyberweapon, and fired at the Cyberleader across the length of the tracking room.

The gun rattled harshly. The silver giant flung up his arms and teetered for a brief moment before crashing forward. The other Cyberman whirled—but Cutler, anticipating his move, had already pressed the trigger a second time.

The Cyberman staggered back against the side wall of the base, smoke pouring from the joints in his suit. Then, like his leader, he fell massively forward, shaking the floor of the base with the impact.

Polly screamed. The other men scattered. Cutler, jumping off the console, strode forward, and immediately took command. He bent down and examined the two dead Cybermen. A thin whisp of smoke was still emerging from their face slits— otherwise there was no sign of life. Severe burns indicated that they had been subjected to an immense electrical charge.

Cutler whirled round, and snapped at the awestruck group which had gathered round him. 'Lost your wits, eh!' He snapped his fingers. 'You men— get with it. All of you.'

He turned to Ben. 'The other Cyberman—where is he?'

'Dead.'

Cutler nodded and pointed at the radio technician. 'Get me Geneva—pronto!'

Polly, still trembling with shock, looked down at the two dead Cybermen. 'Why the hurry? You've killed them all, haven't you?'

'Because, little lady, they'll soon be sending a hell

68

of a lot more over unless we get some action.'

He turned to the other men. 'C'mon, get these things out of here.'

As the technicians started to drag out the dead Cybermen, he turned and strode over to the console, followed by Barclay and Dyson.

The Doctor, standing by the console, faced him for a moment. 'General, I don't think you should have killed them. We might have learnt a very great deal.'

Barclay and Dyson nodded in agreement.

But the General brushed him aside and sat down at the console. He reached forward and opened his box of cigars. Biting off the end of a long black cigar, he spat it out—almost at the Doctor's feet. Then he leant forward and picked up the radio-phone. 'Put me through to Secretary Wigner.'

The feverish activity at International Space Headquarters had continued—and Wigner's jowl, after many hours of uninterrupted work at his desk, was now black with stubble.

The buzzer from *Snowcap* sounded.

'General Cutler for you, sir,' a technician called to him.

Wigner leant slightly over the desk. 'Hello, General, we followed *Zeus Four*'s last orbits from here. A terrible tragedy.'

'That's not the half of it. We've had more visitors since then.'

'Visitors?' Wigner leant back amazed.

'Not human ones, this time. These characters are part man, part robot. They come from Mondas. Three of them broke into the base and overpowered us.'

'I don't follow ... when I last called all seemed well!'

69

Cutler hesitated briefly, and then spoke again. 'I was unconscious when you got the message. The rest of the men here were under threat. They were forced to send you that message.'

Wigner noticed the strong disapproval in the General's tone. 'All right. Forget that now. What's happened to them?'

'We've eliminated them—but there's sure to be more on the way. It's an invasion. They're hostile, strong, and entirely ruthless.'

'This is incredible! If I had heard it from anyone else but you, General, I should not have believed it.'

'You can believe it all right,' the General replied harshly.

Wigner nodded slowly, as if making up his mind. He turned to the other men at the desk. 'We're under attack. Military bases all round the world must be put on immediate alert.'

He turned back to the radio-phone. 'Did you hear that, General?'

'Yeah, loud and clear.'

'Could you deal with another attack with your limited resources?'

Cutler's voice sounded as confident as ever. 'Yep, we can handle them.'

'Good. General, we've got a special task for you. We sent up a single astronaut to help guide Schultz and Williams down.' He paused. 'A mistake, as it turned out. But it was all we could do at the time.'

'When did he go up?'

'He was launched from Woomera just now at 1459 hours.'

'But surely his capsule will be affected like *Zeus Four*?'

'I think we've ... taken care of that,' said Wigner, in his precise, slightly accented English. 'We increased

70

the rocket booster to double and ...'

'O.K.' the General cut in impatiently. 'Do you want us to take over tracking duties?'

'Yes.' The Secretary-General hesitated, as if faced with a difficult task, then went on: 'One other thing. This is a dangerous mission. We needed a brave man. We asked for volunteers.' Wigner paused.

'Sure. So?'

'Your son volunteered.'

There was a long silence.

'General Cutler, are you there?' Wigner turned to the technician. 'Are we cut off again?'

'No, Secretary,' barked Cutler, 'I'm here.' His voice became deeper in tone, almost menacing. 'You sent my son to his death. You realise that, I hope!'

Wigner mopped his brow with a pocket handkerchief. 'We'll get him down, General.'

'With this loss of power?'

'I told you ... his space craft has double the resources of *Zeus Four*.'

The General's voice sounded grim. 'He's sure going to need it!'

'Good luck, General,' Wigner added lamely, and abruptly cut off the radio-phone.

His men had relayed the alert, and were awaiting further orders.

'Now, if Cutler is wrong about these space creatures, we shall have done nothing more than test our global defence system. If he *is* right,' Wigner paused for a moment and looked grimly at his technicians, 'We are probably about to fight the first interplanetary war!'

Cutler turned to his assembled staff. They had listened to his exchange with Wigner over the base loudspeakers.

'O.K., you heard all that. A new capsule is in orbit. Establish contact.'

'But don't you think ...' began Barclay.

Cutler cut him off. 'Think nothing. Act first, think later. Get busy ... all of you!'

The technicians quickly scattered back to their positions at the various consoles.

'And God help the man who falls down on this assignment!' added Cutler.

Flicking over a phone, he spoke to the surviving base guards. 'You guys fell down pretty badly on that last emergency. Fall down on this one and I'll have your hides. Guard the trap door, check the fuel tanks, make sure that any suspicious object on the Polar surface is immediately reported back here. Get moving.'

'What a sickening man!' Polly whispered to Ben. 'He frightens me.'

'Yeah,' Ben nodded. 'Wouldn't want him on the bridge.'

Cutler now spoke into a red phone which led to another extension of the base. 'Anti-missile control? Programme all *Cobra* anti-missiles for imminent launch. Hold at readiness and wait instructions.'

'We'll soon have this place sealed off like a bottle,' he added, turning to the Doctor.

The Doctor shook his head. 'I think you are under-estimating the Cybermen, General Cutler.'

Cutler looked amused. 'Is that what you reckon? Well, you're entitled to your opinions, old man—as long as you keep them to yourself.'

He turned to Ben. 'Here, boy, you seem to be the only guy around here with any real guts. You did well to kill that Cyberman.'

Ben came over a little uncomfortably. 'Didn't have no choice, did I?'

Cutler slapped him on the shoulders. 'Don't apologise boy. He is dead, isn't he?'

Polly turned to the Doctor. 'He's really enjoying all this!'

'What's that?' Cutler looked at the girl.

Polly faced Cutler as bravely as she had the Cyberleader. 'I said you seemed to be enjoying all this.'

Cutler's expression changed immediately. 'Look, girl,' he said quietly, 'I've a personal stake in this emergency. My son has been sent up in a space craft, and you saw what happened to the last one!'

Polly looked at him for a moment, and then looked away. 'I'm ... I'm sorry,' she mumbled.

The General nodded: 'That's O.K. Don't apologise. Just remember.'

One of the radar technicians suddenly cried out: 'General C-C-Cutler.' Everybody turned.

'Yes, what is it?'

'Strong signal on the early warning, sir. Unidentified signal.'

'Well identify it, man!'

'Well it's ...' The radar technician looked confused and pointed to the screen in front of him. 'See here, sir, there are hundreds of them.'

'Hundreds of what?' asked Cutler, striding over to him.

The radar technician pointed to the circular screen —it was covered with little flecks of light.

'Travelling eastwards,' he continued. 'There see?' He indicated with his pencil. 'At an altitude of two thousand miles.'

'Yeah, I see them,' said Cutler. 'But what are they?'

'Spaceships. Maybe up to 250 spaceships, flying round the equator in formation!'

73

9

Z-Bomb Alert!

'What!' Cutler stared hard at the radar technician. He swallowed visibly under the General's gaze, but nodded affirmatively. 'Then,' went on Cutler, 'that means only one thing—more Cybermen!'

He turned to Dyson and Barclay. 'Have you made contact with *Zeus Five* yet?'

'We're still trying, General,' said Dyson.

He looked across at the Radar technician, who called, 'Coming through now, sir. *Snowcap* to *Zeus Five*. How do you read me?'

A new voice cut in on the R/T system, alert and confident. '*Zeus Five* to *Snowcap*—loud and clear.'

Cutler stiffened at the sound of his son's voice, but gave no other visible sign that its owner was more than just another astronaut on a routine mission.

'Are you experiencing any power loss?' Cutler's hand reached for another cigar, nervously twisted it between his fingers for a minute, and then, Polly noticed, carefully replaced it in the box.

Again the voice cut in over the R/T system. 'Hey, that's a voice that sounds familiar ...'

Cutler moved forward in his chair. 'I repeat—any power loss?'

Terry Cutler's voice, recognising the note of command, lost its flippant edge. 'Yes, sir, there's some loss of power when I'm in orbit on the same side of Earth as this new planet. It picks up again on the far side,

74

though. I guess I'm shielded there. Say, what happened to Williams and Schultz?'

Cutler's face set into a mask. The eyes of all his men were on him. 'You won't be docking with them. They ... er ... had some trouble. Our main priority now is to get you down.'

The atmosphere in the Control Room had now gone very quiet. There was no reply over the R/T system—the astronaut was pondering the implications of what his father had said.

Then, as if to get his son's mind off the fate of the other two men, Cutler's voice broke in. 'Son, we have signals down here of a large formation of spaceships. Can you see anything up there?'

After a moment's pause, Terry's voice broke in disbelievingly, 'Is that some kind of gag?' And then, as if the astronaut remembered to whom he was speaking, he continued. 'No, sir. I've nothing to report so far.'

Again Cutler leant forward, speaking almost directly into the mike. 'They're on your orbit, some thirty miles below you.'

'Check!' Again a slight pause, then, 'No, still nothing to report. It's pretty black down there.'

'Keep your eyes skinned and report any sighting immediately—O.K.?'

'Roger, sir.'

'Take care, boy. We'll get you down as soon as we can.' Cutler switched off the R/T mike and turned to the assembled men.

'As I see it, we have three major problems: one, my son has been sent on a foolhardy mission into space, and we have to bring him down. Two, we can expect another visit from these space creatures. Three, that planet Mondas is draining energy from Earth.'

'There is nothing we can do about any of those things.' Dyson, who had said the words almost to himself, suddenly remembered that he had spoken them to the astronaut's father.

Cutler shook his head. 'You're wrong, Mr Dyson. We can do plenty. We can destroy Mondas!'

'But that's impossible!' Barclay broke in.

'Impossible is not in my vocabulary, Dr Barclay.'

'How do you propose to do it then, General?'

'We'll use the Z-bomb.'

After a long silence, Barclay voiced the general feeling. 'But you can't do that!'

'I can—and I will!'

'What about the radiation effect on Earth?' asked Dyson.

'That's a chance we'll just have to take.' Cutler picked up the cigar he had previously discarded. Polly, standing close by, noticed that his hand was no longer trembling. The opportunity for action must have steadied his nerves.

'What exactly is the Z-bomb, General?'

Cutler turned to answer Ben's question. 'It is a bomb that could, if rightly timed, split this planet of ours right in half. Two or three of them are positioned in strategic points around the globe. We have one, and the means for delivering it—square on Mondas!'

Dr Barclay still seemed unable to grasp the full implications of the General's decision. 'You can't use the Z-bomb unless you have instructions from Geneva.'

Cutler sneered. 'Don't worry, fella—I'll get instructions, right here and now.'

He walked across to the R/T console. 'Get me Geneva!'

In the International Space Headquarters, a broad blue band—marking the flight line of the Cybermen space fleet—was inching its way across the surface of the

76

large illuminated wall map. Glowing red dots dotted about the world indicated possible landing sites. Wigner, the strain and tension now showing in his sweating face, was still in icy command of the situation.

The R/T communications man spoke up. 'General Cutler, sir.'

'O.K. Put him through.'

'Mr Secretary?'

'Yes, General?' Wigner leant back in his chair.

'The expected attack—they've been sighted in force.'

Wigner nodded wearily: 'We're getting reports. They're coming in from all parts of the Earth. To make matters worse, the energy drain is increasing rapidly.' He looked down at another batch of teletyped messages which had been thrust in front of him. 'General, you must hold on as best you can.'

Cutler spoke crisply and confidently. 'I think we can do better than just hold on, sir. I'd like permission to take offensive action against this planet.'

Wigner raised his eyebrows. 'What action?'

'The Z-bomb—mounted in the warhead of the Demeter rocket. It's powerful enough to explode Mondas completely.'

Wigner glanced towards his aides—they included scientists, soldiers and two top international civil servants. Without the slightest hesitation, each man shook his head.

Wigner turned back to the console. 'No—we can't take the risk. It might have disastrous effects on Earth's atmosphere! Before taking any action like this we would have to consult our top scientists—which would take time.'

'Respectfully, sir, we're too late. We've already run out of time. This is an emergency.'

'Precisely.' Wigner's thin lips set firmly as he recognised and resented the slighty contemptuous inflection in the General's voice. 'We must know exactly what we are doing.'

'No, sir. No time. We will have to take the chance.'

'Listen to me, General. You must take no precipitous action. And that's an order! It is quite out of the question at the present time.'

Wigner and his aides waited for the expected outburst at the other end of the line—but it didn't come.

But Cutler's voice when it came back to them seemed gentler, more concilatory: 'O.K., Mr Secretary, I understand.'

Wigner relaxed slightly in his chair.

'But, sir ...'

'Yes, General?'

'I do have your authority to take any action that may seem necessary to stop the Cybermen?'

'Yes, General, all I.S.C. military commanders have that authority. You must do all you can.'

'Thank you, sir.'

The general reaction in the Snowcap base was one of relief that Cutler had accepted his superior's decision.

Polly even felt a small sprig of sympathy as Cutler, his shoulders bowed, walked back to his seat at the console. Wigner's decision, whatever it may have meant for the world at large, must surely have meant the end of Terry Cutler. But Polly's sympathy soon vanished as Cutler, a slight smile on his lips, began to speak with as much arrogant confidence as before.

'O.K., gentlemen. Prepare to start the count down.'

'B ... but,' Barclay stammered slightly, voicing the general bewilderment, 'surely you haven't got the authority to use this Z-Bomb. The Director-General just said so!'

'What you heard, Dr Barclay, was Secretary Wigner authorising the use of any step necessary to stop the Cybermen.' His jaw set. 'So get moving!'

There was a moment's silence as the men looked at the General irresolutely. Ben spoke up. 'Yeah, I bet that didn't include using the Z-bomb, though, did it?'

Cutler rose to his feet: 'Those are my orders.'

Ben turned to Dr Barclay: 'Go on, you're the expert, tell him he can't use that bomb. We'll all go up with it!'

Cutler glared at them for a moment, and then spoke quietly, menacingly.

'Ever since you came into this base, you and the old man have tried to poke your noses into things that are not your business!' He turned to the guards. 'Take them out of here and lock them up.'

Polly turned to the Doctor. During the preceeding activity, he had been slumped in a chair by one of the consoles, his eyes looking down at the desk, his face giving no indication of his thoughts. What could be the matter with him?

Polly grasped his arm. 'Are you all right, Doctor?'

The Doctor nodded. 'Yes, child.'

'Then please, please,' she continued, looking desperately round as the guards started to make their way across the room, 'say something.'

The Doctor looked up tiredly and called over to Cutler. 'General! Just a moment. Are you sure this is the only way of dealing with the Cybermen?'

Cutler raised his hand to stop the guards. 'Yes, old man. As they're about to attack *us*, it's the only way I know ...'

The Doctor's voice sounded slightly higher pitched than usual, a little quavery with age. 'There is another

79

way.' He waited until he had everyone's attention, '... to wait! Eh, Dr Barclay?'

'Wait!' echoed Barclay, confused. 'I'm afraid I don't understand you.'

'Well,' snapped the Doctor, 'think, man, think.' He looked around irritably. 'You all call yourselves scientists, don't you? Can't you see it isn't only the Earth that's in danger. Mondas itself is in far greater danger—otherwise why would the Cybermen want to visit Earth? All they have to do, surely, is simply to sit tight and wait until Mondas is replenished by our energy.'

He paused for a moment and looked around him with a little of his old authority.

Finally, Cutler nodded. 'O.K., you've got a point. But so what?'

'Don't you see,' continued the Doctor, 'all the Earth's stock of energy could be too much for this new planet. It could burn itself up, shrivel away to nothing. All we have to do is to wait.'

Cutler intervened sharply. 'Wait until your Cybermen friends get here and take over this planet? No, we're not going to wait, Doctor. We'll *accelerate* the process a little. Mondas will burn up a little sooner—that's all.'

The Doctor's strength seemed to ebb again at Cutler's words, and he shook his head. 'That would be a mistake. A nuclear explosion on Mondas would certainly release a terrible blast of radiation. Enough to destroy all life on the part of the Earth facing it.'

He grasped the console, his face white, and shook his head as if trying to collect his thoughts. Anxiously, Polly took his arm—but he shook her off.

'It might even turn into a sun—a super-nova. It would certainly destroy your son's capsule.'

That's a risk we'll just have to take. As far as the

capsule is concerned, we're going to fuse the bomb and hit Mondas when my son's orbit has taken him to the far side of the Earth.'

The old Doctor shook his head in despair. His fingers nervously tapped his lapels.

Barclay, who had been listening intently to the Doctor, stepped forward. 'General, there is no guarantee of success even if we use the Z-bomb.'

'I'm not arguing,' said Cutler. 'Just do it.'

'Sir,' the radio technician's voice cut in abruptly, 'they're on the move again!'

As Cutler started to walk across to the console, he turned to the guards who were standing by the time travellers. 'O.K., you can take them away now.'

'The girl too?' one of the guards asked, his eyes fixed on Polly.

Cutler looked back briefly, smiled, and shook his head. 'No, she's no menace. I guess you can leave her here.'

As the guards started to lead Ben and the Doctor away, Polly stayed by them, still grasping the Doctor's arm. 'I'm coming too.'

Ben turned quickly and shook his head. 'No you're not, Duchess, you're staying here.'

'But the Doctor?' pleaded Polly.

'I'll look after him. Work on Barclay instead. Get him to see sense,' added Ben in a whisper.

Polly let go of the Doctor's arm and halted irresolutely. Before she could answer, the two time travellers were led out of the room by the guards.

Cutler turned back from the radar screen. 'There's no time to lose. Ready, Barclay?'

Barclay met his gaze for a minute, and then nodded. 'You'll have to be present at the fusing, General. Dyson can't do it without your being there.'

The General nodded. 'O.K., Mr Dyson, let's get

on with it.' As he turned to go, Polly stopped him.

'Can I stay and help?'

Cutler looked at her. 'How do you think you can help, girl?'

'I could make tea or coffee ... or something.'

Cutler shrugged. 'All right. I guess we could all do with some coffee.' He turned back to the radar technician. 'Keep track of those Cybermen. I want to know the moment an attack is imminent.'

10

Prepare to Blast Off

'Doctor! Doctor!' Ben was worried sick. The Doctor seemed to have aged even in the few minutes that they had been locked in the cabin. The guards had thrust them into a room belonging to a couple of the base technicians. It resembled a ship's cabin—with two bunks set one above the other, a built-in wardrobe, chest of drawers, a desk and chair. The Doctor had fallen asleep on the lower bunk almost immediately.

Was it Ben's imagination, or had the Doctor's hair gone a shade whiter and finer during the last few hours? His skin, which looked as transparent as old parchment, was stretched tightly over his prominent cheek bones.

Ben shook his head dejectedly. He began to speak to himself as usual—a habit he had picked up during long night watches at sea.

'Better let the poor old geezer sleep. He looks all done in.' He looked around the cabin, then got up, walked over to the door and tried the handle. Locked. Parts of an electric iron were scattered about the table —one of the technicians had obviously been repairing it. Beside it was a small tool kit—pliers, wire cutters, screwdrivers, etc. Ben eagerly picked up the tools, and started work on the door lock.

After a quick examination, however, he gave up in disgust and flung the tools back on the desk. 'What's the use? They didn't have locks like this back in the 1970s.'

He sat down dejectedly in a chair, and began to rock it backwards. Suddenly, something on the ceiling caught his eye.

Just above one end of the upper bunk, a large square grille—part of the air conditioning system—had been let into the ceiling.

Ben measured it with his eye. How large was it? Taking a sudden decision, he sprang to his feet, picked up one of the screwdrivers and, carefully avoiding the sleeping Doctor, scrambled on to the upper bunk.

Dyson and Cutler entered the silo room. Cutler looked around him curiously. Although as base commander he made a monthly tour of inspection, the silo room was not a place to linger in. In spite of the many nuclear technology courses which Cutler had attended, he had little real understanding of how to assemble and launch a nuclear weapon. 'All a General needs to know is the location of the "fire" button,' was how he usually explained away his ignorance. It was his job to make the decisions—and up to the scientific egg-heads to understand the technology that made it all possible.

The oblong-shaped room, which had been painted a neutral mid-green, contained a complex array of pipes colour-coded in red, blue, and yellow. Along one wall ran a bench containing electronic equipment and several large cylinders connected by pipes to the bomb itself. A large hatch led through to the tall, two-storey-high Demeter rocket in the firing tube. From there, the bomb could be placed directly into the 'pay-load' area.

However, it was the Z-bomb itself which caught—and held—their attention.

It looked like a smooth cylinder with rounded ends,

approximately sixty centimetres across by one hundred and twenty centimetres long. Over the Z-bomb hung a steel lifting cradle, which was connected to the ceiling by thin chains. Around the top half of the room a gallery with a railing projected three feet out from the wall. It was reached by a ladder from the floor of the silo room, and provided access to the various system control panels set at intervals around the room.

Cutler, followed by Dyson, walked over to the bomb, and stared down at it for a moment. Various labels, stencilled in bold white letters which read ISC PROTOTYPE A, had been fixed to the grey surface. At one end of the bomb another label read No 1 FUSE LOCK, and at the other No 2 FUSE LOCK.

Cutler listened to the hiss of the vacuum pumps. The metal beneath him vibrated to the powerful hum of the large dynamos.

'O.K., Dyson, hurry it up. What are we waiting for?'

'We've last minute checks, sir.' He pointed to the gallery where two engineers with clipboards were checking the dials and ticking off a column of figures.

Cutler nodded and stepped back. 'The sooner we get this baby loaded and into the rocket, the sooner our problems will be solved.'

Dyson, his head averted, nodded and mumbled something. Cutler smiled. 'I'm glad you at least agree with me.'

Dyson looked up anxiously. 'If we get this away, do you think we stand a chance, sir?'

'I don't work out chances in advance. It doesn't pay. As far as I'm concerned, we've no alternative.'

'But the Doctor could have been right—it might be safer to wait.'

Cutler removed his cigar. 'Wait nothing. History is littered with guys who waited. And where did they get? Nowhere!'

'But what about the radiation effects? I mean, nothing is known ... this bomb could ...' He stopped. Cutler noticed his hands were shaking.

'You know, I've never heard you say so much before. What's the matter, Dyson—chicken?'

Dyson shook his head quickly and looked down at his clipboard. No, not exactly.'

To his surprise, Cutler put a hand on his shoulder. 'Come on, man, admit it. When it comes to the Z-Bomb, I'm chicken—we all are! But I'm also scared for my son. That's why we're going to send this thing off.'

He looked up at the engineers. 'Come on, fellas. Hurry it up, will you, time's short. You want to book a good seat in the Control Room ready for the fire-cracker display, don't you?'

The men grinned down at him and nodded.

Dyson felt more confident now. 'O.K., we can start now, sir.'

Cutler watched as Dyson and the two engineers started working on the bomb. First, they opened two lockers—widely separated at either end of the room—with special keys, and took out identical cylindrical fuses. Positioning themselves at opposite ends of the bomb, they began to screw them firmly into place.

This done, the rotary click switches at the ends of the fuses were rotated in readiness for the number combination which Dyson now stood in readiness to dictate. He glanced from one engineer to the other. 'Ready? Right! Seven, two, five ...' The deadly combination, number by number, was being set ...

In the main control tracking room, Barclay was leaning anxiously over the communication technician's shoulder. 'Well?'

The R/T technician shook his head. 'Still can't raise Lt. Cutler, sir.'

'Keep trying. Tell me the minute you hear from him.'

Barclay walked back to the console, his brow furrowed, thinking deeply. He became aware of Polly standing by his desk. She had placed a tray with coffee, tea, and soft drinks right in the middle of his papers.

'Get that out of here,' he snapped.

'I'm sorry.' She indicated the tray: 'Tell me what you want first.'

'Oh!' Barclay looked at the display before him: 'Coffee, I suppose.'

'Are you trying to get in touch with General Cutler's son?' Polly asked, as she poured out his coffee.

Barclay shook his head irritably. 'Just keep your mind on the coffee, will you?'

Then, realising what he had said, he looked up at her: 'I'm sorry, that was very rude of me.' He smiled wryly. 'You must be scared stiff with all this happening.'

Polly nodded. 'If Mondas turns into a sun and pours out deadly radiation, how much would it affect us?'

Barclay looked away as if reluctant to tell her the worst. 'I don't know—of course it might not affect us at all.'

'That wasn't what you said just now.'

Barclay shrugged despairingly: 'Let's face it, no one's completely sure what could happen.'

'But you do have some idea?'

'I suppose,' Barclay looked at her almost guiltily, 'the radiation could affect us. There's bound to be some— and probably considerable, loss of life. The Earth's vegetation will suffer very badly over a period of years.'

Polly, who had been drawn before by Barclay's gentleness, drew back a little. 'And you're prepared to let this take place?'

'What else can I do? General Cutler holds all the cards. He makes the decisions.'

Polly looked around her for a moment, then leant forward across the desk, and whispered, 'Can't we wait, though—fight off the Cybermen until Mondas is destroyed? It might mean the end of Cutler's son, of course, but it would be one life against millions.'

The tall physicist looked at her miserably and shook his head. 'What can I do? If I don't follow the General's orders, he's quite capable of going ahead without me. He's a very ruthless man.'

'Couldn't we pretend to follow his orders—but make sure the rocket doesn't go off!'

Barclay looked at her with fresh hope, the idea beginning to take root ... Suddenly, they heard Cutler's voice on the other side of the tracking room.

Polly moved back rather too quickly, as if caught in a conspiracy. But Cutler didn't seem to have noticed. He was speaking to the radar technician. 'Anything to report?'

'Yes, sir. A signal on the screen—about here.' He indicated with his finger. 'Fifteen hundred miles north north-east, altitude fifteen zero. It's been stationary for the last ten minutes.'

Cutler peered at the screen for a moment. 'Keep a close watch on it. Report to me the instant it starts moving. Any more word from my son?'

Barclay came to the General's side. 'We can't seem to raise him, General.'

'What?' His eyes searched for the R/T technician but, before he could speak, the radar technician broke in urgently: 'That blip, it's moving, sir. Coming in fast, course o-one-five.'

'Where's it heading?'

'Straight in here, General.'

'The Cybermen again?' asked Barclay.

88

Cutler nodded: 'Must be.'

'Do we use the anti-missile battery this time?' asked Barclay. Cutler shook his head. 'No, I've a better idea. We'll let them land. Then ambush them with their own weapons.'

He looked towards the console by the door where the Cybermen's captured weapons were still laid out in a row, then tapped the R/T man on the shoulder. 'Put the whole base on red alert. Stand-by.'

'Right, General.' The R/T technician leant forward and spoke into the mike. 'Now hear this. All base to red alert stand-by. Repeat, all base to red alert stand-by. Enemy landing imminent. Report to your stations.'

Cutler picked up the phone and dialled a number. 'Security Major? Put your three best marksmen under snow camouflage and issue them with the captured Cyberweapons. Report on your R/Ts when you are in position.'

Cutler turned back to Barclay. 'How long to count down?'

Barclay glanced at his watch for a moment. 'Ten minutes.'

'They'll be here by then. We'll have to hold them off first, then proceed with the launching.'

A buzzer sounded harshly. 'Well?'

Dyson's voice came over the loudspeaker system. 'The bomb's in position in the rocket, sir. Will you check it now?'

'Yeah, just got time before the battle commences.' He turned and strode rapidly out of the room.

Polly turned excitedly to Barclay. 'Now's our chance,' she whispered.

'What?' Barclay turned, startled.

'To see Ben—he may be able to help. We must do something to stop that rocket.'

Barclay hesitated, glancing indecisively from Polly to his seat at the control console.

'Quick,' continued Polly. 'It's our only chance—while the General's out of the room. Come on—hurry before it's too late.'

Trying to appear inconspicuous, she picked up the coffee tray and walked towards the door. Barclay hesitated for just a moment and then followed her.

In the cabin, Ben had removed the grille and edged his body half way up through the exposed ventilation shaft. 'Lucky we don't get much grub on the TARDIS —I'd never get through this on navy rations!'

Suddenly, he heard the cabin door open. Legs waving wildly, he tried to wriggle out of the shaft.

'Ben!'

He turned quickly: to his relief it was Polly!

She ran across and peered into the Doctor's face. He still seemed to be fast asleep. 'How is he, Ben?'

Ben eased himself down from the top bunk. 'Cor, I'm glad to see you, Polly.' He nodded towards the Doctor: 'He seems pretty fair.'

Barclay entered the room and closed the door behind him and Ben turned quickly, on his guard.

'It's all right, Ben, Dr Barclay's going to help us.'

'Great! Good work, Polly. What can we do to stop this rocket, then?'

Barclay looked towards the door, and then moved closer to the two time travellers. 'It can be immobilised quite simply—if one can get into the rocket silo, that is.'

'Can't you?'

Barclay shook his head. 'Cutler suspects me already. It's under constant guard. If I or any of my staff try to tamper with the controls, we'd be discovered immediately.'

'Is there any other way then?' asked Ben.

'I don't know.' Suddenly, he caught sight of the open ventilation shaft, and then looked down at Ben. 'Can you get through that?'

Ben nodded. 'I was just about to scarper when you came in. What about it?'

'I designed this part of the base. That's the main ventilation shaft. It leads through to the silo room—and the bomb!'

Ben nodded. 'I get you. Maybe I could do something. Would I need a radiation suit?'

'No, the silo room is screened.' He thought for a moment. 'But there's a guard outside and there's sure to be an engineer or two checking the systems inside.'

'Couldn't we distract them?' queried Polly. 'Get them outside somehow?'

Barclay nodded. Yes, perhaps.'

Waah! Waaah! The harsh bray of the station alarm, sounding similar to a submarine alert, echoed through the base. Polly jumped. 'What's happened?'

'The Cybermen must have landed. I must go.' Barclay turned to the door.

'No,' pleaded Polly. She grasped his arm. 'Don't you see, this is your chance?'

Barclay thought for a moment, and then sat down again. 'You're right. Here.' He motioned to Ben and, turning to the desk, picked up a pencil and pulled a sheet of paper towards him. 'This is what you'll have to do.'

Ben watched as Barclay started to draw a plan on the graph paper. He glanced down at the tool kit which Ben had used earlier on the door. 'You'll need these.' He pointed to a section of his diagram. 'Unscrew this panel. Inside there are four small plugs.

91

Take out any of them, snip off a pin, and put it back.'

'What will that do?' queried Ben.

'The fuel pump pressure will drop to zero at blast off.'

'You mean the rocket engine won't work? But won't they spot it? And correct it?'

Barclay shook his head. 'Not in six months. That's not the sort of fault they would look for.'

Outside on the Polar surface, the wind had dropped, the moon had come out and a strange, unearthly silence dominated the crackling, cold landscape. The moonlight added a silver sheen to the Antarctic plains, giving them a dreamlike, shimmering appearance.

The long, ugly, torpedo-like shape of the Cybermen's spacecraft broke the silence as it gently came to rest.

A moment later, the revolving red light began to fade, a slight whirring noise was heard, and part of the side section slid back. The first of the Cybermen stepped gingerly down into the Polar snows.

He looked around him, weapon at the ready— but all that was visible were the slopes leading up to the small cluster of chimneys and slight hump that marked the Polar base.

On the far side of the base, the Cyberman noticed the small, square shape of the TARDIS, and for a moment levelled his weapon in that direction—but there was no visible movement.

Reassured, he turned and pressed a signal button on his chest unit. One by one, the other Cybermen climbed down from the spacecraft.

At the entrance to the Polar base, the three guards detailed to ambush the Cybermen were waiting, rod-like Cyberweapons at the ready. They had made a rough 'blind' out of the snow with a white tarpaulin cover. With the exception of a small slit, they were completely invisible.

They watched as the Cybermen advanced across the snow.

In all, the guards counted twelve of the silver monsters, their tall figures glinting in the moonlight as they tramped in perfect unison through the dry powdery snow towards the base.

Nearer and nearer they came. In spite of the intense cold, the two men on either side of the Security Major were sweating with tension. When would he give the order to fire? There was something implacable and terrible in the steady, machine-like tread of the Cybermen ...

The leading Cybermen had now marched to within ten feet of the blind.

'FIRE!' the Major shouted to his men. Almost simultaneously, the rattle of the three Cyberweapons rang out. The guards chosen for the duty were the three crack shots on the base—but it was unnecessary at such close range.

The three leading Cybermen jerked up their arms, staggered backwards, and fell. Behind them, the other Cybermen looked wildly around for their opponents.

Again, the three guards fired with unerring accuracy.

Three more Cybermen dropped.

The other Cybermen, still unsure where the attack was coming from, began to retreat.

Again the guards fired at the retreating figures, and three more Cybermen jack-knifed into the snow.

The remaining three turned and ran wildly through the snow back towards their waiting spacecraft.

The guards fired again, but the distance, and the strange ghostly Polar moonlight seemed to confuse them. Only one of the three remaining Cybermen was hit. The other two reached the safety of the spacecraft.

The Security Major flung off the white cover of the blind. 'O.K. Get their weapons. Then back inside—fast!'

While the Major clambered down into the base to report, the other two men walked quickly over to the dead Cybermen to collect their prizes. One of the Cybermen had fallen on top of his weapon. Nervously, the guard kicked the lifeless giant aside, and snatched up his booty.

Ben, inch by effortful inch, was heaving himself along the base ventilation system.

The shaft, a narrow, square tunnel with protruding metal joins, dug into him as he wormed his way along. Every few feet, the tunnel was dimly lit by a shaft of light which penetrated a grille. Ben wondered how visible he was through these close-mesh grilles, and made every effort to pass them as quickly as possible. His clothing had torn on the projecting screws, and his elbows and knees were raw and bleeding.

He paused. Ahead of him, he caught sight of a square intersection of two tunnels. Three ways: which one to follow?

He eased himself back to the previous grille and, by the light filtering through the mesh, examined the piece of paper Barclay had given him. Again he moved forward checking the stencilled numbers over the intersections. FIVE, SIX, SEVEN. Number five was the one to follow. He turned awkwardly and dragged his body at right-angles into the new tunnel. His face and singlet were wet with sweat. In spite of the warm breeze which was blowing along the shaft, and the short distance he had travelled, his arms and legs were beginning to ache intolerably ...

Ahead he saw three grilles set close together—as described by Barclay. Cautiously, he put his eye to the thick mesh, looked through—and sighed with relief. The rocket silo! He had arrived exactly where Barclay had indicated on the sketch plan.

Looking down into the room, Ben could see that he had reached a grille set over the gallery. He looked across, and froze! An engineer with a clipboard was working almost directly opposite!

His hand felt for the four flynuts that held the grille in position, and started to loosen them. The hum of the powerful dynamos would prevent his activities being heard; he was also invisible through the grille—until, that is, it was removed. But where on earth was Dr Barclay?

He removed the top right hand flynut, the left, then began to loosen the lower ones. The grille began to sag outwards. One touch, and it would fall through —leaving the way clear. He looked across at the engineer to see if he had noticed anything, then saw that the man was looking down and nodding to somebody below.

By pushing his cheek against the warm metal top of the shaft, Ben could just make out the floor of the silo room and the now empty bomb cradle. The bomb had been loaded into a hatch leading directly into the rocket launching tube and the waiting *Demeter* rocket. He saw an engineer fasten the large bolt arrangement that closed the square safe-like door of the hatch. Beside him stood Dr Barclay.

As Ben watched, almost holding his breath, he saw Barclay lead the man away, then look up and beckon to the engineer opposite Ben.

After what seemed an age, during which time Ben's

neck was horribly cramped by the awkward angle at which he had to hold his head, he saw the engineer climb slowly down the metal ladder, and follow Barclay and the other man out of the room.

The door closed behind them and, for a few precious minutes, the room was Ben's. He pushed the grille out with his hand, then, as it clattered down, eased himself through and landed on the narrow gallery. He stretched his cramped muscles in relief, and brought out Barclay's instructions.

Following the directions, he started tracing a line of twisted multi-coloured lead wires through the rocket launching controls. His fingers stopped opposite a panel labelled: PUMP SERVO LEADS.

Bringing out his screwdriver, he began to unscrew the panel ...

In the tracking room, Cutler had been watching the ambush of the Cybermen relayed by the TV camera. As the last of the Cybermen climbed back into their spacecraft, he raised the stub of his cigar, smiled, and screwed it triumphantly into the ashtray. He turned to the R/T technician.

'Tell them they did a great job. Have the Cyber-weapons brought down to the guard room.'

He stretched himself, easing his muscles after the tension of the last few minutes. 'Barclay,' he called. He looked around—but the tall Australian physicist was nowhere to be seen.

'Dyson,' he snapped, 'where is Dr Barclay?'

'I don't know, sir—he wasn't here when I got back.'

'Where could he have gone at this time? He's needed right here!'

Dyson, busy with his own calculations, looked up again. 'Er ... perhaps he went down to the rocket silo.'

'Rocket silo!' Cutler's face changed, his jaw set. 'We'll see, shall we?' He strode over to the door.

In the long corridor outside the silo, Barclay and the two engineers were in conversation. Outside the sound-proofed room the roar of the mighty dynamos was even louder, and the three men only became aware of Cutler's presence when he was standing beside them.

He pushed the two engineers aside and confronted Barclay. 'Just what are you doing here, Dr Barclay?'

Barclay's jaw dropped. His nervous glance gave him away. 'We were just checking my ...'

Without a word, Cutler grasped him by the tunic, thrust him aside, opened the door of the silo room, and rushed in. Immediately, he caught sight of Ben's head inside the panel.

Dropping his hand to his belt, Cutler drew his heavy automatic, and levelled it at the intruder. Taking careful aim, the General's finger tightened on the curved trigger ...

As he fired, Barclay pushed his arm aside. The gun boomed, echoing round the metal walls of the silo room—but the bullet missed Ben, struck the metal panel and ricochetted off.

Holding Barclay aside with his other arm, Cutler levelled the automatic at Ben again.

'O.K., sailor,' he ordered, his voice rasping above the hum of the machinery, 'get down here—at the double!'

For a second, Ben hesitated, torn between his uncompleted task, and almost certain death from Cutler's gun.

The rocket had to be stopped—whatever the cost.

He turned back to the exposed wires, but Cutler, in one swift and incredibly agile leap for so large a man, reached the ladder, and grasped Ben's ankle.

Ben gave a cry as he felt himself being pulled backwards. He tried to grab the rail but his head struck the metal platform. He slumped unconscious from the gallery and landed in a heap at the bottom of the ladder.

Barclay saw Cutler raise the gun again. 'Stop!' he yelled. But Cutler replaced it in his holster and turned to the guard who had just entered.

'Get him along to the control room.' He turned to the engineers. 'You two get back on that rocket.'

Cutler turned to Barclay. The man backed away. 'Look, I can explain,' Barclay's voice was shaking.

Cutler glanced at him with contempt. 'Don't bother. You're coming with me right now. I need you. We'll talk about this after the rocket has been fired.'

He turned to the guard who had lifted the unconscious sailor. 'Have his companions brought along, too. Seems I can't rely on anyone else to keep an eye on them.'

'You're treating him like a criminal,' Polly shouted. Ben, his head bleeding, was slumped, still unconscious, in a chair by the main console.

The Doctor was sitting beside him, wide awake but silent. Polly was bathing the back of Ben's bloody head.

Cutler turned to her. He had posted guards with drawn carbines on either side of the time travellers. His automatic rested on top of the console. 'As far as I'm concerned, he is a criminal! I'm warning all of you, if that rocket doesn't take off for Mondas, and if my son's life is in jeopardy because of him, I shall take the law into my own hands.' He looked across at Barclay. 'And that goes for you too, Dr Barclay. You'd better do a damn good job on this launching—or else!' He turned to the other technicians. 'O.K., start the count down.'

Barclay looked down at the console. 'Preliminary checking is not complete, General. I'll inform all concerned when ready.'

Cutler nodded abstractedly and walked over to the R/T set. He glared at the operator. 'I thought I told you to keep trying to contact *Zeus Five*? Get with it!'

The R/T technician spoke tremblingly into the microphone. '*Snowcap* to *Zeus Five*, *Snowcap* to *Zeus Five*. Come in please.'

After a crackling of static from the loudspeakers, Terry Cutler's voice broke in. '*Zeus Five* to *Snowcap*. Receiving you loud and clear. Over.'

Cutler's dark, heavy-set face lightened suddenly. He leant over, shoved aside the R/T technician, and grabbed the mike. 'Hello, son. Any sign of those spacecraft in your vicinity?'

'No, sir. I'm all on my lonesome up here.'

'Well watch it, they move mighty fast.'

'Only one question. When are you going to bring me down?'

'We can't do it yet. You'll just have to hold on. We're going to deal with the planet Mondas first. How are things with you?'

'I guess the capsule's getting a little slow at the controls.'

'What about the power?'

'It loses, then picks up again.'

Cutler nodded. 'Yeah, Mondas is affecting it—we'll get you down as soon as we can.'

For the first time the voice of the young astronaut showed a sign of strain: 'Thanks. Can't be too soon for me!'

Cutler's face looked concerned. 'Good luck, boy—switching off now.'

The astronaut's voice came through almost as an aside. 'Luck! I'm going to need it.'

As Cutler slowly replaced the mike, Barclay's voice cut in.

'All systems ready to proceed with count down.' His voice echoed through the loudspeakers. 'Barclay speaking. Please check in. Silo Control?'

'Check,' replied the silo engineer.

Polly crouched by Ben. He was coming to; his eyes were half opened—but he seemed dazed. She looked towards the Doctor. 'Doctor, can't we do something?' But the Doctor still seemed half asleep. He shook his head as if lost in a day-dream, and didn't reply.

'Gantry team?' queried Barclay. The answer came: 'A1 O.K.!'

'Fire control?'

'Check!'

'Ben!' Polly said urgently. 'Speak to me, please.'

'Um?' Ben peered round the room, trying to focus. 'Who is that? Who's talking?'

'Keep your voice down,' whispered Polly.

'P ... Polly? What happened?'

'Look,' she glanced round the room, 'I'll tell you later.'

Cutler and the team were now too deeply engrossed in the count-down to pay attention to the three time travellers.

'Radar vectors check?' queried Barclay.

'Check,' came the voice. 'T minus one fifty and counting,' said Barclay.

Polly whispered in Ben's ear again. 'Did you manage it?'

Ben held his head in his hands: 'I can't seem to hear you, Poll. My head's splitting apart.'

'Ben, you must remember. Please try and think!

Did you manage to do what Dr Barclay told you?'

'I just don't know!'

Suddenly another voice cut in through the loud-speakers. 'Silo here. We have a fault on range computer. Check all circuits.'

'Stop the countdown,' ordered Barclay.

Polly put her mouth close to Ben's ear. 'Does that mean they've found the fault?'

'Dunno,' said Ben, confused.

Suddenly, Cutler became aware of the implication of the last report. He rose from his seat at the console, and pointed the heavy black pistol at Barclay:

'Exactly what is the matter with the range computer?'

Barclay's face went pale. He shook his head. 'Only a minor fault, General.' He spoke into the mike. 'Holding at T minus one and thirty-five.'

Cutler leant forward, his gun pressed against Barclay's chest. 'It'd better be minor.'

'Fault clear,' confirmed the voice from the loudspeaker.

Cutler looked round, then slowly relaxed, replacing the gun on the bench. Barclay took out a handkerchief, mopped his brow and looked over at Ben. Then he turned back to the mike.

'Proceed with countdown, counting T minus one point three five from—now!'

'Oh, Ben!' cried Polly. 'Don't say it will fire—after all you've done.'

But Ben could only shake his head in confusion. Had he or hadn't he? If only he could remember!

11

Cybermen in Control

'T minus thirty seconds.'

Polly grabbed Ben's arm and whispered to him. 'We'll know if you succeeded in just a few seconds.'

The whole tracking room was electric with tension. The Z-Bomb, which was capable of splitting the Earth in half, had long been held as the so-called ultimate deterrent. Nobody, least of all the men manning the base, had thought that this terrible weapon, the most destructive invented by mankind, would ever be used.

Now the unthinkable was happening. In a few seconds the hatches at the top of the silo would open outwards in the snow to reveal the cannon-like mouth and long deadly rocket—destination Mondas!

'T minus twenty seconds.' The voice of the technician reading the seconds off the countdown clock shook slightly as the long hand moved relentlessly towards the moment of blast off.

'T minus ten seconds.'

'T minus five seconds.'

The entire base personnel had now taken their cue from Dyson, who had put his hands over his ears, and was bracing himself for the shock as the giant rocket motors ignited deep beneath them. Only Cutler held himself aloof from the excited apprehension of the others, standing erect and soldierly as ever, watching the countdown clock.

The shock never came.

After a long moment's pause, the technicians uncovered their ears and stared incredulously at the clock—now silent. The countdown had finished; the automatic ignition should have taken place; twenty tons of deadly payload should have been roaring— visible on their large monitor screen—up from the base. Instead, nothing had happened. Why?

In the sudden silence, Polly, unable to contain herself any longer, leaped to her feet and clutched Ben round the neck. 'Ben—you made it! It hasn't worked. Now we've all got a chance to live—even the Cybermen!'

Beside her, the tall figure of Cutler froze, as he realised the implication of her words. He turned towards Ben, and spoke slowly, gratingly: 'Your new friends, the Cybermen, may have a chance of life— but not you, sailor.'

He turned to the Doctor who was sitting beside Ben. 'Nor you, old man.'

The Doctor had been lost in thought throughout the entire countdown. Now he rose to his feet and Ben and Polly watched in amazement as the mask of age and extreme fatigue fell away. The failure of the Z-Bomb had galvanized him. He seemed to have recovered his former strength and resilience.

'It seems, sir,' he said to Cutler in his mannered, slightly old-fashioned English, 'that your plan has been foiled. The rocket has not gone off.'

But Cutler only gave him one contemptuous glance and turned away to consult with Dyson.

'Are you all right, Doctor?' asked Ben. His head, although it still ached from the fall, had now cleared.

'Yes,' added Polly. 'What's been happening to you, Doctor?'

'I'm not sure, child. An outside force of some kind, perhaps? This old body of mine is wearing a bit thin.'

'A bit thin?' asked Polly anxiously.

'Yes,' replied the Doctor. 'It's nearly time for a change ...'

Then, seeing her worried look, he continued, 'Oh, don't worry, I'm all right for the time being, I expect ...'

He was interrupted by the strident voice of General Cutler, who had turned away from Dyson, and was now speaking, automatic levelled, to the unfortunate Dr Barclay.

'The rocket was sabotaged with your help, Dr Barclay. I'm going to give you one more chance to get it off the ground.' He raised his pistol and aimed at the physicist's head. 'Or I'll shoot you right here and now.'

There was a nervous flurry in the room as the technicians moved hurriedly back out of range.

Barclay, although highly nervous, looked up, his face set with a desperate courage. 'I can't fire this rocket now—and neither can you.'

'How long will it take to re-fuel?' asked Cutler.

'Quite long enough.'

After a long silence, Cutler spoke again. 'I see!' He nodded as if to himself. 'If that's the way you want to play it.' His brow furrowed and the time travellers could see the veins on his neck tighten. His finger began to apply pressure to the trigger. Barclay closed his eyes.

'No! No!' screamed Polly, running forward.

Her voice shattered the horrible suspense within the tracking room. Cutler, as if returning to reality, shook his head. He steadied himself, relaxed his hold on the trigger, and lowered the gun.

'Get up!' he ordered.

Barclay quickly rose to his feet.

'Now get over there with the rest of them.' He

pointed to the time travellers. Barclay moved over and stood beside Ben, who had risen nervously when Cutler picked up the pistol.

Cutler, without taking his eyes off Barclay, Ben and the Doctor, spoke out of the corner of his mouth to Dyson. 'Try to get Lt Cutler once again.'

Dyson sat down in the chair of the R/T operator, and picked up the earphones. The R/T operator looked towards Cutler. 'We've been getting a signal, sir.'

Cutler nodded. 'Put it through.'

Dyson pushed a switch forward and a voice, broken, distorted, but still unmistakably that of Cutler's son, began to speak.

'Hello, *Snowcap*. Do you read me? Hello, *Snowcap*.'

Cutler strode over and picked up the address mike. 'Hello, son, reading you, but very weak. Speak up.'

'I'm bawling my head off—now. I'm tumbling badly. Little control left of capsule. Must speak fast.'

'Go ahead, son.'

'This new planet . . . something strange is happening. It seems to brighten up like a sun—then darken again.'

The Doctor started forward. 'There, you see—I told you it couldn't absorb much more energy.'

Cutler did not appear to have heard the Doctor's interjection. He was listening too intently for his son's next words.

The radar technician's voice broke in over the curtain of static from the loudspeakers. 'Sir, sir.' His voice was high-pitched, urgent. 'Cybermen spaceship on approach path—heading right here.'

'SHUT UP—ALL OF YOU!' Cutler shouted at the top of his voice. 'Terry,' he called into the mike, 'are you still there?'

Lt Cutler's voice was coming over more and more

faintly. 'Hey ... control going again ... energy loss severe ... like being on a switchback ... can't seem to ...'

The set cut out with a sudden click. The silence, as the static faded, was disconcerting.

'Son!' shouted Cutler, shaking the mike and looking round desperately, 'hello—do you read me?' He turned to Dyson: 'Get that signal back!'

Dyson shook his head. 'It's gone, General. It could be a power failure.'

For the first time, Cutler seemed to lose control. His sweating face was distorted with anxiety; his shoulders slumped forward. He looked older than a man in his middle fifties. 'Keep trying. For heaven's sake, keep trying.'

The radar technician's voice broke in again. 'Sir, Cyberman ship on descent now.'

The technicians rose to their feet in alarm. The room became a babble of speculation. Only Cutler seemed oblivious to the news. He was bent over the seated Dyson, watching him as he manipulated the wave bands, trying to catch a signal from the capsule. Cutler's voice was almost pleading. 'Come on, fella, give it everything you've got. There must be some signal.'

Dyson shook his head reluctantly. 'No good, I'm afraid. It's quite hopeless.'

Barclay shouted across to the General. 'Sir, the Cybermen will be landing at any moment. Don't you realise ...'

'General!' The Doctor added his voice to try and gain Cutler's attention—but he simply ignored them all.

'The enemy, General—they're landing,' shouted Barclay.

The word 'enemy' suddenly seemed to get through

to Cutler. He straightened up from the R/T control console and turned towards Barclay. 'The enemy,' he was speaking slowly, eyes staring, mouth slightly open, 'I'll tell you who the enemy is—you, Dr Barclay, are the enemy.'

The R/T technician stood up and pointed towards the screen. 'The Cybermen, sir. They must have landed!' He indicated the screen, empty of blips—but Cutler ignored him.

Brushing all the technicians aside, he started walking towards Barclay and the time travellers, holding his automatic pistol loosely at his side.

The technicians scattered before him. Cutler's face was twisted, frightening, almost demented.

Barclay turned desperately to the soldiers. 'He's gone off his head. Can't you see? Disarm him!'

But Cutler's authority at the base was absolute. The men clutched their carbines nervously and watched as if paralysed.

Cutler raised his gun and indicated the three men one by one. 'You,' (he pointed at Barclay) 'you,' (he pointed at the Doctor) 'and you,' (he pointed at Ben) 'are the culprits. Because of your actions my son is dead. I'm going to deal with you personally.'

The General levelled his pistol, his face impassive. His gun moved from side to side for a moment, as if uncertain which one to shoot first—then it stopped at the Doctor. His finger tightened, his eyes narrowed as he aimed ... Polly began to scream hysterically.

A shattering noise came from outside the tracking room—the crack of rifle shots followed by the grating rattle of Cyberweapons. The doors burst open inwards, and a guard staggered through, his tunic smoking, dead before he collapsed on the floor of the tracking room.

The guards inside levelled their weapons—but before they could take aim across the crowded room, the tall figure of a Cyberman appeared.

General Cutler wheeled round, and aimed his automatic at the Cyberman. The technicians ducked beneath their consoles as Cutler fired.

The bullet hit the Cyberman's front armour and ricocheted off with a slight clang. Then the Cyberman fired back.

The rattle of the Cyberweapon was followed by a moment's silence. Had the General been hit? His gun was still levelled: he seemed to be trying to focus ... Then, as the others watched horrified, the tell-tale wisp of smoke crept from the collar of his tunic, his eyes clouded, and the gun dropped from his fingers.

Almost in slow motion, the General's long body fell forward to the floor in death.

'Silence!' The harsh voice of the Cyberman filled the room. 'Anyone who moves will be killed instantly.' He walked slowly and ponderously towards the centre of the tracking room. Behind him two more Cybermen entered, weapons levelled.

The men in the room seemed this time frozen to the spot—like statues. The new Cyberleader, wearing a black helmet, loomed over them all with terrifying authority.

The Doctor stepped forward. Immediately the Cyberleader swung round to face him, weapon levelled. The Doctor held up his hand.

'Do not shoot. I wish to speak to you.' He turned and pointed to Barclay and his two companions, who were still flanked by the two armed guards. 'We owe our lives to you.' He pointed down at the dead General Cutler. 'This man was about to kill us.'

Krang, the new Cyberleader, gestured at the guards with his Cyberweapon. 'Drop your guns. They are useless against us.'

Without hesitation, the two guards flung down their carbines and raised their hands.

Krang pointed to the Doctor and his companions. 'You four go over there and join the others.'

The Doctor, Ben, Polly, and Barclay moved backwards with the two guards towards the end of the tracking room where the Cybermen were herding the base technicians.

'That's gratitude for yer!' Ben had recovered his wits and voice. 'We save their grotty planet—for what?'

'Shh,' whispered the Doctor. But it was too late. The Cybermen had heard. Krang turned to face them. 'Saved Mondas? We do not believe you. We have seen a rocket missile aimed at Mondas.'

Again the Doctor stepped forward, hands grasping the lapels of his long black cloak. 'That is so. And we have prevented it being fired at you. We have therefore helped you. Now I suggest you help us in return.'

Ben shrugged his shoulders and turned away in disgust. 'You're wasting your time talking to them geezers.'

But the Cyberleader raised his hand for silence. 'What do you ask in return for this?'

The Doctor looked at him, his head tilted back, his authority—now that Cutler was gone—pre-eminent in the room. Even the technicians and guards hung on his every word, seeming to recognise that he was their new spokesman.

'Your planet is finished. It will disintegrate. We know that is why you have come here. So why not stay and live in peace with us?'

The impassive black mask of the Cyberman stared back at him. 'We will confer,' conceded Krang. 'Keep your places. Anyone who moves will be killed instantly.'

He motioned to the other two Cybermen and, together, they walked to the control end of the tracking room, and gathered behind Cutler's console.

Dyson turned nervously to the Doctor. 'Can we trust them?'

Ben shook his head gloomily. 'You kidding? Course we can't!'

'Tch!' The Doctor gestured nervously with his long hands. 'It is all we can do. We must play for time.'

The Cybermen now turned back towards the men.

'Well?' asked the Doctor. 'What have you decided?'

'We cannot talk while that missile is still aimed at Mondas. It must be disarmed first.'

The Doctor held up his hand. 'One moment.' He turned and beckoned Dyson and Barclay towards him. As they put their heads together, he whispered, 'Can you disarm the rocket?'

Barclay nodded. 'Why yes, Doctor, but ...'

The Doctor nodded. 'Good, this will give us time.'

Ben had also caught the Doctor's remarks, and now nodded excitedly. 'Time for Mondas to burn itself out?' he asked in a hoarse whisper.

The Doctor gave him a quick nod, flicked his finger to his lips for silence, and turned back again. 'We have agreed to your terms,' he called across the tracking room. 'We will remove the warhead from the rocket.'

'It must be removed below ground level.'

For answer, the Doctor turned to Barclay. The physicist nodded. 'It can be moved to the radiation room—the deepest room in the base.'

'That will do,' replied the Cyberleader. 'And to make sure you do this, we will take a hostage.' He pointed to Polly. 'That girl will go to our space craft. You will go with the others to the rocket,' he said to Ben and Barclay.

'Doctor!' exclaimed Polly, frightened.

But the Doctor only shook his head. 'We must do as they say—go, child.'

'Not ruddy likely!' Ben blurted out. He turned to the Cyberleader. 'If you want a hostage, what about me?'

'All the men are needed to help with the warhead.'

'Oh yes?' Ben moved forward, threateningly. 'Now look here. I say you're not going to take her ...'

The Cyberleader raised his gun.

The Doctor stepped forward, grasped Ben's arm and eased him back. 'Ben, please let me handle this.'

'But, Doctor,' protested Ben, 'we can't let Poll ...'

'It's all right, Ben,' Polly stepped forward. 'Let the Doctor decide.' She swallowed nervously. 'If the Doctor wants me to go ... at least it will be a new experience. I've never seen the inside of a Cybercraft.'

The Doctor turned to the Cyberleader, his voice sharp and controlled. 'Do you give us your word that she will be returned safely when the bomb is stowed away?'

'Yes. I give you my word,' replied the Cyberleader in his icy monotone.

To her surprise, Polly had been blindfolded for the trip across to the spacecraft. Before leaving the base, she had put on one of the thick fur parkas worn by the guards. Now, seated in a small cabin aboard the Cybercraft, her blindfold removed, she felt extremely grateful for the thick Polar clothing.

The chair to which she had been fastened by metal clamps across her waist and around her wrist, reminded her of an electric chair. She shuddered at the thought.

The Cybercraft seemed to be unheated. Then she remembered that the Doctor had said that the Cybermen, being creatures of plastic and metal, not flesh and blood, would have no need of heat—they were impervious to heat and cold alike. But what about their human hostage? The South Pole ground temperature must be thirty or more below zero!

As the cold began to chill her, she tried to move her arms—but the clamps held her firmly in place. She struggled and began to cry out. Suddenly, the door slid open and one of her tall silver guards stepped into the room. Realising it was useless to plead, she decided to bluster.

'Look,' she shouted indignantly, putting on what Ben would have called her best 'Duchess' voice, 'I agreed to act as hostage. I gave you my word I wouldn't escape. Isn't that enough for you? It's freezing here. I'm flesh and blood—not like you. I'll freeze to death in minutes.'

Without answering, the Cyberman advanced towards her. She shrank back, and screamed slightly, as his helmet almost brushed her face. The Cyberman pressed a button on his chest unit; a flash shot from his helmet to her temple, and Polly fell forward unconscious.

The Cyberman looked down at her for a moment, then turned to the temperature control on the wall. He hesitated for a moment. What temperature would be needed to keep alive someone from Earth? Then he sharply twisted the control.

As Polly slept, warm air began filtering into the cabin. The Cyberman had obviously been ordered to keep his captive alive. But for how long?

12

Resistance in the Radiation Room

'Geneva calling. South Polar base. Geneva to South Pole. Are you receiving me?'

The voice of the Geneva technician boomed through the loudspeaker, filling the tracking room. The Doctor was sitting in Barclay's chair. Behind him stood the massive figure of Krang, easily dominating the whole room. Without moving, Krang spoke to the Doctor.

'Answer them.'

The R/T technician indicated the radio-phone on the Doctor's right.

'Into here?' asked the Doctor.

The technician nodded.

'Hello, Geneva. *Snowcap* base here.'

To his surprise, his own voice echoed through the loudspeaker. The R/T technician hurried over, and pulled a switch down.

'You were speaking into the public address system for the base. This is the one to use,' he said.

'Thank you.' The Doctor nodded. 'Hello, Geneva,' he repeated.

'Geneva here. Secretary Wigner to speak with General Cutler.'

The Doctor glanced involuntarily over to the place where Cutler's body had been—but it had been taken away by the guards.

'The General is ... not here at the moment. I ... have been ...'

He suddenly became aware of the cold metal shaft of a Cyberweapon pressing against the side of his neck. '... left in charge here temporarily.'

'Who is that speaking?' asked Wigner.

The Doctor shook his head impatiently: 'There's no time to discuss that now, sir.'

'Tell General Cutler that there have been mass landings of Cybermen in many parts of the world. We have had no report for ...'

Suddenly, cries and screams came over the loudspeaker system—followed by the dreaded rattle of a Cyberweapon.

The space technicians glanced at each other in horrified silence.

'Geneva,' called the Doctor urgently. 'Geneva—are you there? What has happened? Secretary Wigner?'

After a moment's silence, a new voice came over the loudspeaker. It was harsh, metallic, unmistakably similar to the other Cybermen—but with a slightly deeper tone.

'Geneva is now ours. The Earth has been taken over by Mondas. Only scattered pockets of resistance remain, and these are being dealt with.'

'Remove yourself,' rasped the voice of Krang behind the Doctor's ear.

He rose from his seat, and Krang sat down in Barclay's chair. The Cyberleader leant forward and spoke into the mike.

'South Pole take-over completed.'

Again, the voice of the Cyberleader came over the loudspeaker. 'This is Cyberleader Gern. I am now in control of the Earth. No time must be wasted. Mondas is in great danger. We cannot absorb much more energy from Earth.'

The Doctor nodded his head in confirmation.

'You must proceed with your second objective.'

'We are proceeding according to plan,' confirmed the flat tones of Krang.

'Report to me as soon as you are ready,' the Cyber-controller said. 'We must have time to evacuate.'

There was a click and then silence.

The Doctor, who had been listening to the exchange, gasped as a thought struck him. He leant forward. 'I don't understand your friend. What does he mean: evacuate? How can you return to Mondas now?'

The Cyberleader looked stolidly ahead. 'We will not discuss our plans with you.'

'Oh!' commented the Doctor. He raised his sharp eagle profile and looked down at the Cyberleader—as if pitting his will and intelligence against that of the man of steel. 'Just what is your plan?'

No reply.

'It's obvious then, isn't it?' the Doctor continued. 'Your second objective is the destruction of Earth!'

Quickly, the Doctor turned, ran across and shouted into the mike:

'Barclay! Ben! Do not help them. Do you hear me?'

Before he could explain further, the steel hand of the Cyberleader clamped over the Doctor's, flung it aside and pushed back the switch with such violence that it almost broke in his steel grip ...

The base radiation room, a long, low, vault-like chamber, lined with lead to prevent the escape of radiation, was situated beneath the rocket silo. The Z-Bomb had now been taken out of the rocket warhead, into the silo room, and from there had been lowered by cradle through a trap door to the floor of the radiation room.

Beside the Z-Bomb, a series of hexagonal manhole covers led down to a small nuclear reactor pile which provided the base with light, heating, and power.

The reactor rested on nothing but the solid bedrock of the Antarctic.

Ben, Barclay, Dyson and one of the technicians were easing the bomb on to a trolley in readiness for its removal to the lefthand side of the room.

They looked like spacemen in their bulky white anti-radiation suits and perspex head vizors.

'Do not help them.' The Doctor's voice boomed through the loudspeakers.

They looked up at a small monitor screen showing the tracking room. The Doctor had turned to Cutler's console and depressed the PA switch. Again, his voice came over the loudspeakers.

'They mean to use the bomb to blow up the Earth!'

The PA system abruptly clicked off and, on the monitor screens, they saw the Doctor flung back against the wall with one sweep of the Cyberman's arm. The Cyberleader leant over the console and slammed his fist down. Abruptly, the monitor screen blanked out.

Ben turned to the others, his voice muffled through the mouthpiece of the radiation suit. 'Did you all hear that?'

'Of course,' replied Barclay. 'It all makes sense now,' he continued on bitterly. 'We've allowed ourselves to be fooled by them.'

Dyson nodded. 'We just set them up nicely. Cutler was right, wasn't he? We should have used the bomb on them—whatever the consequences.'

Barclay shook his head. 'That might easily have started off something far worse.'

'Worse!' Dyson raised his arms as far as his bulky suit would allow. 'We're about to be blown up, along with the entire population of the Earth, and you talk of something worse happening!'

'Give over, mate.' Ben spoke sharply. 'What he means is while there's life, there's still hope.'

But Dyson moved away in despair. 'I've a feeling we've just signed our own death warrant.'

Barclay turned away from the bomb, silent and pre-occupied.

Ben looked from one to the other. An idea was beginning to form. 'Half a mo'. I'm beginning to get the drift of all this.'

'Marvellous!' said Dyson sarcastically.

'Yeah,' continued Ben angrily. 'Well you might at least listen! I haven't heard any bright suggestions from you two brains!'

Barclay turned back. 'Sorry. Go on.'

'Any idea how strong these Cybermen are?' asked the sailor.

Barclay shrugged. 'A rough idea.'

'Well, they can lift a man like ...' Ben looked around and lifted a spanner, '... this spanner, right? They are five, maybe ten, times as strong as we are. They are also pretty advanced geezers, right? Way ahead of us in science and technology?'

Dyson snapped irritably. 'What's all this got to do with it?'

'Plenty. If they're so strong and clever, why do they want us to do the work for them? They could shift this bomb in half the time. What's more, you must have noticed that the Cyberguard always stays outside this room, watching us through that door.' He pointed to the Cyberman's helmet, which was visible through the thick glass observation panel. 'Why?' Ben asked.

'This is just a waste of time,' mumbled Dyson.

But Barclay grasped his arm. 'No, wait. I see what

you're driving at. They use us because they can't handle the bomb themselves.'

'Yeah, that's it!' said Ben excitedly. 'The point is, why? You're the scientist.'

Barclay thought for a moment, then smiled. 'Of course, it's quite clear. Don't you see, Dyson? The reason could be that they are afraid of radioactivity!'

Dyson looked towards the door, and then back at the others. He nodded a little reluctantly. 'Could be!'

'Well don't let's just stand here, let's prove it,' said Ben. 'Let's get this one inside here. See what it does to him. Come on, lie down on the floor.' He turned to the waiting technician. 'You, too. All of us. Play dead.'

'This is ridiculous,' grumbled Dyson, but Barclay caught hold of him and pulled him to the ground.

'It's worth a try,' he whispered. 'Lie still.'

Ben looked at the three men now lying motionless on the floor, their limbs spread, eyes closed behind the face vizors. 'Lovely!'

He walked towards the door, pulled back the opening lever and swung it open. His eyes met the blank stare of the Cyberman.

'You,' said Ben, pointing to him. 'Help us! Come in here quick. Something's happened to the others.' As he spoke, he sagged, grasped at the door frame, and staggered back into the room.

For a moment, the Cyberman paused suspiciously and looked through the open doorway. Then he caught sight of the prostrate, apparently dead, scientists. Ben slowly crumpled to his knees; his head bowed.

The Cyberman cautiously stepped inside: one pace; two paces. After three paces he stopped dead. Ben looked up, a whirring noise from inside the Cyberman's chest unit had begun; the lights on his front

118

unit were flashing wildly—like a pin-ball machine. The Cyberman stiffened, his hand opened; the Cyber-weapon dropped.

Quick as a flash, Ben sprang up and grabbed the gun. The Cyberman was completely immobile; frozen as a lump of Polar ice. Ben pulled on the silver giant's arm, swung him around and, with one great shove, sent him crashing out of the room. He slammed the door, and threw the bolt. Behind him, the others started to rise.

'What on earth did you do that for?' said Dyson, getting to his feet. 'We could have escaped.'

'You're still not using your nut, chum. Escape! To where? We're O.K. right where we are.'

Barclay looked more hopeful. 'And they can't set off the bomb while we defend this room?'

The sailor nodded. 'Yeah, that's what I figure. All we've got to do now is sit tight and wait for Mondas to shrivel up like the Doctor said. We've got 'em.' For a moment he grinned at the two men triumphantly—then his face fell.

'But they've still got the Doctor and Polly!'

In the tracking room, Cyberleader Krang had just watched the tail end of the action in the radiation room. He had turned the monitor sets volume control up to catch Ben's last words.

The Doctor was standing, menaced by one of the Cyberguards. He looked over at Krang. 'There, gentlemen. Stalemate I would say, wouldn't you? Now perhaps we can talk!' He placed his fingers together in a characteristic gesture.

The Cyberleader turned, and replied angrily. 'You forget—we can do what we like with all of you.' He indicated the technicians. 'And, of course, the girl.'

'Of course,' the Doctor nodded. 'But that won't save your planet, will it?'

Krang thought for a moment, then stepped forward and picked up the address mike. 'I will speak to them.' He looked across at the TV monitors, depressed a switch, and began speaking to the small figures of Barclay, Ben, Dyson, and Haynes on the screen.

'Listen to me. This close proximity of our two planets mean that one has to be eliminated for the safety of the other. The one to be destroyed will be Earth. We cannot allow Mondas to burn up. If you help us, we will take you back to Mondas with us. There you will be safe.'

'Oh yeah!' Ben shouted up towards the mike in the radiation room. 'For how long?'

'No,' Dyson whispered. 'Don't antagonise them. It could be our only hope.'

The watching Cybermen saw Ben push Dyson aside and look up directly at the monitors. 'The answer is no! We will just sit tight here until your planet breaks up. Now you'd better release the Doctor and Polly and send them down here. You'll need our help when Mondas is gone!'

The Cyberleader's voice began to speak with greater intensity. 'Mondas will not explode.' He turned to one of the other Cybermen. 'Take the old man out to the spacecraft.'

'No,' pleaded the Doctor. 'I must stay here. You need me.'

'The Cybermen do not need anyone's help,' snapped Krang. He gestured and the Cybermen standing by the Doctor grasped his arm and led him from the room.

Krang turned back to the monitor screen. 'Now! We give you three minutes to start fusing the warhead. If you fail, you will never see your friends again!'

Dyson turned to the others. 'It's hopeless. We must do as they say.'

'It could be a bluff,' said Barclay uncertainly.

'Yes,' Ben agreed. 'Perhaps we should find out?'

Barclay shook his head. 'We must keep to our plan and sit tight. There are millions of lives at stake.'

'But Polly and the Doctor?' said Ben desperately. 'There must be something we can do!' He looked round and, before the others could stop him, rushed over to the TV monitor and ripped out the lead wires from the camera lens and microphone.

'What on earth did you do that for?' asked Dyson. 'Now they cannot communicate with us.'

'Yeah,' said Ben, turning back. 'They can't spy on us either, can they? I've got a plan ...'

Aboard the Cyberman spaceship, the Doctor was now seated beside Polly in another of the Cyberchairs. The Cyberguard was clamping the broad silver bands across his waist and arms.

'Doctor,' said Polly, 'can't you do anything?'

The Doctor shook his head and looked pointedly at the Cyberman. They waited until he had turned and left the room. 'At least, my dear,' replied the Doctor, 'they have allowed us some heat. They obviously mean to keep us alive.'

'But there's something else. A few minutes ago they started up some kind of engines.'

'Engines?' queried the Doctor.

'Yes. Listen!'

The Doctor became aware of the low throbbing vibration coming from the heart of the ship.

'It wasn't here before. They're not taking off, are they?'

'No.' The Doctor shook his head. 'Wait! Listen! Feel the vibration. I don't believe it is the engines.'

Their bodies were vibrating with the rest of the Cybership.

'Mondas must be causing this.'

'Mondas?' queried Polly.

'This spaceship gets its energy from Mondas. It must be absorbing too much.'

'Do you mean it will blow up, Doctor?'

'I don't know, child. I really don't know ...'

The men in the radiation room were having an urgent counsel of war. Ben had raised a bench on end to block the door observation window. For the first time since the advent of the Cybermen, the men felt that they were not being watched.

Ben pointed to the Z-Bomb. 'What's it weigh then?'

Dyson smiled. 'You're not thinking of trying to carry that around, are you?'

'Who's asking you, laughing boy?' Ben retorted. He turned to Barclay. 'Can it be shifted?'

Barclay shook his head. 'It would be an impossible job, I'm afraid. To use it as you would intend to use it, that is.'

'Well,' Ben looked round, 'what *is* movable in this room? Something that a bloke could carry?'

'Nothing,' replied Dyson decisively. 'You're wasting your time and ours.' He looked at his watch. 'The three minutes is nearly up anyway.'

Ben turned to Barclay. 'Think, man!' He went over to the reactor manholes and pointed. 'Is there anything radioactive down there?'

'Yes,' replied Barclay, coming over. 'Of course! The base nuclear reactor that supplies all the power!'

'Well, what's it like?' asked Ben excitedly. 'I've

never seen a nuclear reactor. Is there anything we could move by hand?'

'Well,' Barclay kneeled down, 'it's powered by thin uranium rods. They could be carried a short distance. But they are highly radio-active. It would be a ticklish operation.'

'Ticklish or not, we've got to do it. It's our only chance. Come on.' Ben looked around. 'How do you get these things up?'

Dyson came forward. 'Have you all gone mad?'

Ben turned on him angrily and Dyson, although bigger built, backed away. 'We're the sane ones, mate! You really think those Cybermen mean to let us live?'

'They gave us their word,' said Dyson.

'Word!' Ben laughed. 'They just said anything they thought we'd listen to. They've got no feelings, remember. *They* told us that. So what's to stop them?'

Dyson fell silent. Ben shook his head.

'You might as well face it, mate. Your number's up either way—so why not at least try to find a way out of this mess?' His tone changed. 'We need your help—alright?'

For a moment Dyson looked undecided, then nodded.

Ben turned to Haynes, the technician. 'How about you?'

'Count me in.'

As they spoke, Barclay was already levering up the first manhole in preparation for the difficult—and dangerous—operation of lifting the uranium rods.

In the tracking room, the large circle of the Tenth Planet now almost filled the huge telescopic screen. The Cybermen watched it in silence. Mondas was violently alternating from light to dark. The Cyberleader looked up at the wall clock.

'Our planet is nearing saturation point,' Krang said. 'Switch on the monitor. Their three minutes is up. We must hear their decision.' He gestured to another black helmeted Cyberleader.

Cyberleader Jarl switched the TV monitor on—but the screen remained blank. He turned to Krang. 'There is no picture.'

He switched on the PA connection to the reactor room—but there was no 'on' light. 'They have cut themselves off.'

'Then,' retorted Krang ominously, 'we must use other methods.'

Ben flung open the door of the reactor room. He had checked the observation room—the corridor was empty. The irradiated Cyberman had either left or been carried away by his comrades.

'All clear,' he called. 'But hurry it up. It won't take them long to find out that we've cut off the TV monitor.' He stood aside to allow Dyson and Haynes, each carrying a nuclear rod, through into the corridor.

They held the dark grey rods, which were three feet long, by long pincers at arm's length. Behind them Barclay carried a small geiger counter—one of the emergency sets permanently stored in the reactor room. The Australian physicist watched the rapidly ticking machine.

'Steady,' he called. 'Steady. Hold them away from yourselves. Gently does it now. Very, very gently.'

He turned to Ben. 'Stand by the emergency power switch. The lights will be going any second now.'

The men could hear the hum of the great dynamos set beneath the base begin to run down. The lights faded.

Ben raised the large lever and thrust it into position. Immediately the whine of the dynamos rose again in pitch. The neon lights brightened to normal.

Dyson looked back at Barclay nervously. 'You realise that there is only an hour's lighting and heating on the emergency batteries? Then we shall freeze to death?'

'If this doesn't work—you won't have to worry about the cold!' Ben joked grimly.

He pointed along the corridor. 'While it's clear— get around the corner. Dyson—hide in one of the rooms up there in the corridor. When the Cybermen pass you, come out behind them. Haynes,' he indicated the other stretch of corridor, which made a right hand bend just outside the reactor room, 'you'll find a room along this corridor.'

'I'll draw their fire,' Ben continued. 'When you hear this gun,' he held up the Cyberweapon abandoned by the Cyberman in the reactor room, 'start moving forward.'

Ben and Barclay watched as the two men lumbered awkwardly away down the corridors in their bulky radiation suits, gingerly carrying the deadly grey rods in front of them.

Ben turned to Dr Barclay. 'Think there's enough radiation in the two rods to trap them?'

Barclay looked at the geiger counter. 'Should be.'

'Let's get back in here then,' said Ben.

They re-entered the radiation room and closed the door.

Inside the tracking room, the second Cyberleader, Jarl, had mounted a pair of cylinders—very like a skin diver's compressed air kit—on his back. A black, corrugated pipe led to a nozzle held in front of him.

Krang inspected Jarl. 'We will not use this gas unless we have to. We need them conscious.'

The Cyberleader unstrapped a small black transmitting unit used to keep in contact with the Cybership, and placed it on the desk. He then unclipped the Cyberweapon held underneath his chest unit.

He turned and beckoned to the other Cyberman. As the captive technicians watched, the Cybermen filed out after Krang and Jarl.

There was a moment's relief in the tracking room after the Cybermen had left. The R/T technician jumped up, ran over and tried the door. It was locked. He turned back to the others.

'We could break it down!'

Rogers, the base's senior engineer, shook his head. 'They'd soon hear us and return. And then there'd be more killing.'

'We've got to help them.' The R/T technician pointed at the blank screen of the reactor room. But again Rogers shook his head.

'That sailor's a very resourceful man—they've obviously got a plan of some kind. If we start acting on our own initiative, it could upset it. The best thing we can do is sit tight.'

Ben had opened the reactor room door slightly, and was looking along the corridor. He saw the tall frame and black helmet of Krang turn the corner and darted back inside, still leaving the door slightly ajar. 'They're coming—quick—behind the door!'

As the heavy tramp of the Cybermen resounded along the metal-floored corridor, the two men positioned themselves behind the door. Outside, the heavy footsteps stopped. Krang's voice rasped through the slightly open door.

'Your three minutes is up. What is your decision?'

The two men stood stock still without answering.

'We shall be forced to kill you,' went on Krang. 'We will give you one more chance to come out and yield us the Z-Bomb.'

'Come in and get us,' yelled Ben.

Krang nodded to Jarl, who thrust the gas nozzle through the crack in the door. The Cyberman turned the control knob to full, and the gas hissed out in a steady stream.

Inside, as the thin stream of white gas started spreading through the doorway, Barclay started to cough. The gas was beginning to seep through the breathing filter on his helmet.

'Keep your position,' whispered Ben. He ran over to the far wall, levelling his Cyberweapon at the doorway. 'Now,' he called.

Barclay leant forward, grasped the door lever and, keeping safely behind it, swung the heavy, lead-covered door wide open.

Ben saw Jarl outlined in the cloud of white gas in the corridor. Hardly stopping to aim, he levelled the Cyberweapon and fired.

The rattle was deafening in the radiation room. Through the clouds of gas, Ben saw the tall Cyberman drop the nozzle, raise his hands in the air, and stagger back.

Quickly, the agile sailor leapt to one side as Krang and the other Cybermen fired their weapons through the radiation room door.

Ben reached Barclay, now almost doubled up behind the door. The nozzle of the gas cylinder continued to spurt out a white stream of gas. Barclay gasped in Ben's ear. 'I can't hold out much longer.'

Ben, his eyes and nose also streaming from the tear-gas, croaked, 'Where are Dyson and Haynes?'

The Cybermen were having difficulty seeing in through the heavy white cloud. A Cyberman stepped

127

over Jarl's body—but Krang stopped him. 'No. That is what they want. We shall be immobilized if we enter the radiation room. Let the gas do its work.'

The Cyberman stepped back. The whole corridor was now full of the smoke-like gas but, behind the Cybermen's backs, the white-clad figure of Haynes was approaching stealthily, holding the nuclear rod before him.

Suddenly, his head began to swim with the tear-gas. He coughed violently. The end Cyberman wheeled round and made out his figure through the swirling clouds of gas. For a moment he paused, irresolute. Clad in the radiation suit, with its square helmet, Haynes looked not unlike another Cyberman ...

The Cyberman called to Krang, who turned and saw the technician advancing down the corridor. The Cybermen were beginning to shake from the effects of the radiation which emanated from the out-thrust nuclear rod.

'We must leave,' Krang said.

The Cybermen turned to escape down the other corridor—but the figure of Dyson loomed through the fog-like gas, a second nuclear rod held in front of him.

The Cybermen were now shaking uncontrollably from the effects of the radiation. Krang raised his Cyberweapon and turned from one man to the other, trying to make out a target. He aimed at Haynes, whose shape was now clear through the gas, and fired.

The technician gave one cry, staggered, and with the last of his strength, thrust the rod towards the Cybermen before collapsing forward in the corridor.

Ben, choking and almost insensible from the gas, reeled out into the doorway and aimed point blank at the Cyberleader. His gun rattled. Krang slowly turned, his weapon still levelled and, for one moment, Ben thought he was going to fire.

Like a forest giant, the dead Cyberleader slowly toppled forward, crashing on to Jarl's body.

Ben ran forward, felt for the control wheel on the gas cylinders, and quickly turned them off.

As the gas began to clear, he saw that the other three Cybermen had frozen into position; their weapons pointed uselessly downwards. Lights were flashing on their chest units. As Ben raised the Cyber-weapon their chest lights died out and, one by one, the Cybermen teetered and fell.

Dyson appeared, stepping gingerly over the Cyber-bodies. He was still carrying the nuclear rod.

'Quick,' said Ben, coughing from the effects of the gas. 'Get Barclay out of here.'

Dyson carefully placed the nuclear rod in the corridor and helped Ben drag Barclay away along the corridor. As they passed Haynes, they glanced at him quickly—and shuddered. His eyes were staring upwards in death.

They staggered up the stairs at the end of the corridor, ripped off their helmets and gulped in the clear air!

13

The Destruction of Mondas!

Uncertain as to what was happening, the men in the tracking room watched with apprehension as the door began to open. They braced themselves for the re-appearance of the Cybermen but, to their surprise, Ben and Dyson staggered in supporting Barclay between them. They were still wearing the lower part of their radiation suits.

They placed Barclay on his seat at the console and leant against it, drawing in long, shuddering breaths.

The technicians crowded around excitedly. Dyson told them of the fight in the corridor and the defeat of the Cybermen. 'Get back to your desks,' he continued. 'The emergency is not over yet. There are those rods out of the nuclear reactor—see they get put back.'

'Yeah,' added Ben, 'and don't forget they've still got the Doctor and Polly.' Stripping off his radiation suit, he began to walk towards the door.

'Wait!' Barclay, who had recovered a little, was sitting up and calling him back. As the new commander of the base, he spoke with a new sense of authority and purpose. Ben halted and turned to him.

'If you try to tackle the spacecraft single-handed, you haven't a chance. We don't know how many more Cybermen there are.'

'So?' asked Ben.

For answer, Barclay pointed to the Cyberleader's transmitter which had been left on the top of the console. 'There's the thing they use to contact each other.'

Ben shrugged and lifted up the black box—it resembled a portable transistor radio. 'I don't know how to work it!'

'Do anything,' said Barclay. 'Send out a signal—draw them here.'

The other men within earshot murmured their disapproval. Dyson, who had been testing the various life support systems to ensure that none had suffered in the recent emergency, turned to him. 'Is that wise?'

'If they take off in their ship,' said Ben, 'we'll never see the Doctor and Polly again.' He picked up the Cyberman transmitter.

'Hold on.' Dyson rose to his feet. 'You may bring them all back again.'

'That's a risk we've got to take,' said Ben. He looked down at the many buttons on the Cyberman transmitter. His hand hovered indecisively, then he started pressing them.

Immediately, the small transmitting light began to twinkle; the set emitted a high-pitched buzz.

'That should do it!' said Ben. 'It sounds like some sort of warning signal, anyway. How long do you reckon we've got before they arrive?'

Barclay rose to his feet. 'We'd better get ready for them.'

'I'll go down and get the weapons,' volunteered Ben. As he spoke, the tracking room lights started to flicker and dim down.

'What's happening?' said Ben.

'The emergency power supply must be running out. Why haven't they got those rods back in? We'll freeze to death here within twenty minutes without the base reactor.'

The lights had now become so dim that—apart from

131

the glow from the various monitor screens—the long low room had become a collection of dim black shapes.

'We can't face them in the dark,' called Ben. 'Are there no torches here?'

'Yes,' said Barclay. He was feeling his way over to the side wall.

Behind him, Dyson flicked the PA switch connecting the console mike to the reactor room. 'Philips, Barker,' he called, 'can you hear me? Why aren't those rods back in?'

Ben turned; all he could see of Dyson was a vague shape outlined against the blue projection screen.

'You're forgetting, mate,' he said. 'We ripped the wires out, didn't we?'

Dyson cursed. Barclay turned round, flashlight in hand, and switched it on. He turned the light beam towards Ben. 'I've got one for you.'

As Ben moved to get it, Barclay shone the light towards the door. The beam flicked over the rows of consoles, the faces of the waiting technicians and, by the door, three silent silver figures ...

For a moment, the torch shook in Barclay's hand. The voice of one of the three Cybermen rang out: 'Further resistance is useless. Drop your weapons!'

As the Cyberman spoke, the lights began to brighten back to full power.

The tired, strained men turned to face the third Cyberman invasion of the Snowcap Polar Base.

'You fool!' screamed Dyson. He turned to Ben. For a moment Ben thought he was about to break into tears. 'I warned you not to activate that thing.' He pointed to the black Cyberman transmitter box.

Barclay shook his head wearily. 'No, some kind of warning must have gone out earlier—at the time of the fight. They'd never have made it here in time otherwise.'

'Silence!' snapped the voice of one of the Cybermen. 'We have been patient with you. But this will not continue. You have fought us and destroyed many of our number. Your bomb must be activated immediately, otherwise we shall commence killing every single man in this room.'

He pointed at Ben. 'Starting with this man.'

The Cyberman raised his weapon and aimed it at the sailor. But they were interrupted by a high-pitched shout from the R/T technician. He had been staring at the large screen, and adjusting the controls of the radio-telescope to bring it into sharp focus.

'Look at Mondas!' he cried.

Everyone in the room, men and Cybermen alike, turned to look at the screen. The planet's alternation from light to dark had now speeded up to such a rate that it seemed to visibly flicker—like a slow-running movie projector showing a silent film. The land masses and the dried-up seas that so closely parallelled those on Earth were still visible—but something new was happening!

'Fantastic!' Dyson exclaimed. 'It seems to be ... melting!'

As they watched, huge fissures and cracks appeared. Trickles of white-hot lava were running from the cracks and down the face of the planet. The whole surface seemed to be bubbling and erupting, creating thousands of minor volcanoes. The land masses began distorting and running together. The glare from the planet was now so intense that they had to shield their eyes to look at it.

'It's falling to bits!' exclaimed Ben.

'The end of Mondas,' Barclay's voice rang out triumphantly. 'The Doctor was right.'

In their excitement, they had forgotten the Cybermen standing behind them. The cosmic drama on the huge screen had taken all their attention. Now Ben turned to see how the Cybermen were reacting to the end of their planet.

'Look!' he called. The men turned to look at the three silver figures.

Like their planet, the Cybermen seemed to be suffering a visible change. Their arms had dropped; the Cyberweapons had fallen to the floor; each was teetering slightly on his feet.

As the men watched, they slowly began collapsing down on one knee, then the other. Finally, they pitched forwards on to the floor.

Ben ran over and picked up one of the Cyber-weapons—but it was unnecessary. The plastic ac-cordian-like chest units of the Cybermen were already turning soft—as though the plastic was melting. Cracks appeared, and a grey, evil-looking foam began coursing out.

'They're shrivelling!' said Ben.

Behind him, Dyson calmly gazed down at the three Cybermen. 'They must have been completely depen-dent on power from Mondas. They had no time to transfer their power unit to Earth.'

They turned back to look at the Tenth Planet—but it existed no longer. A huge shifting amoeba-like corona of gas surrounded its few solid remaining seg-ments.

'It's turned into a super-nova,' said Barclay. 'In half an hour it will disperse to the far corners of the universe.'

They watched the distorted flare of gas grow fainter and fainter as it spun away from Earth. The technician struggled vainly to keep it in the telescope lens.

Abruptly, the R/T system spluttered into life and the voice of Terry Cutler came through, ringing loud and clear of all static. '*Zeus Five* to *Snowcap*. Are you reading me? Come in, please. *Zeus Five* to *Snowcap*. Are you receiving me?'

'Quick,' Barclay turned to Dyson. 'Answer him.'

Dyson leant over and spoke into the mike. *'Snowcap* to *Zeus Five*—hearing you loud and clear.'

After a moment's pause, Cutler's voice came over. 'Say, what's happened? Where have you been?'

'Here, give it to me,' said Barclay.

Dyson moved aside and Barclay sat down at the console. *'Snowcap* to *Zeus Five*. Report your fuel position.'

'O.K. Everything's suddenly working normally. How about getting me out of here?'

'We are on emergency power at the moment. We will handle your splash-down as soon as we get full power back.'

He turned to Dyson, relieved to be back at work once more. 'Start checking on the base's main units.'

Dyson nodded and hurried back to his console. All over the room, the men had now resumed their normal positions and were starting the complicated splash-down procedure.

Ben looked from one to the other in bewilderment. 'Hey,' he said, 'what about the Doctor and Polly? They may have killed them.'

But both men, utterly engrossed in their routine jobs, were oblivious to his words.

Without waiting for a reply, Ben rushed over to the dead Cybermen, picked up one of the fallen weapons and dashed out of the door.

Again the base loudspeakers crackled into life. *'Snowcap*, Geneva here.'

Immediately Barclay leant forward, pressed the switch down and responded. 'Hello Geneva—*Snowcap* here—fully operational.'

Wigner's voice came over. *'Snowcap*. Who is that? Dr Barclay?'

135

'Yes. We're getting full power back. The danger is apparently over. What is the global situation?'

'The Cyberman menace has ended all over the world. We're just picking up the pieces. Let me have a full report as soon as you can.' Wigner's clipped voice cut off abruptly as he moved on in his round-up of the I.S.C. bases.

Barclay leant back for a moment and grinned across at Dyson. 'We certainly will!' he said, speaking to no one in particular. 'Did you hear that?' He laughed ironically for a moment. 'He wants a full report.' He raised his hands in the air in a desperate gesture. 'Where exactly do we begin?'

The Cybership had also been affected by the energy loss. The vibration had died away—and a great flash had lit up the forward compartment—followed by the unpleasant smell of burning plastic—as Mondas disintegrated. The Doctor and Polly were struggling to get out of their bonds—but the silver bands held them.

'If you could only reach that control.' The Doctor nodded over the wall beyond, where the controls activating the bands were situated.

Polly tentatively stretched out one of her long legs, but it was quite impossible to reach it from her chair. 'It's no use, Doctor,' she wailed despairingly.

Already the Arctic cold had begun to seep into the abandoned spacecraft. The bright alloy walls seemed to be loosing their lustre. It was as though several years of slow corrosion were being telescoped into as many minutes. The only lights still working were the phosphorescent emergency lighting panels.

Polly saw something. She held her breath. The door was opening slowly. 'Doctor! Doctor! Look!' she called.

The Doctor jerked his head around. The muzzle of a Cyberweapon was poking through the doorway at them. The sudden shock seemed to prove too much for the Doctor. His head slumped forward, eyes glazed, just as Ben stepped into the room.

'Ben!' Polly burst out in a great explosion of relief. Illogically, she seemed almost angry. 'Did you have to give us such a shock? And what took you so long?'

Ben grinned down at her. 'Sure you want to hear it right now, Duchess? Well ...' He leant back against the wall. 'There's nothing I like better than a captive audience, so here goes ...'

'Don't you dare!' Polly squealed. She nodded over to the wall unit. 'The controls are over there. Just press them—and make it quick!'

'Will do.' Ben glanced at the Doctor—but the Doctor didn't look up. He went over to the wall and pressed the button. The straps receded into the chair and Polly jumped up. She started rubbing her cramped wrists.

'Oh boy!' Polly said. 'I'm frozen. I'll never grumble about the TARDIS' heating system again after this!'

But Ben wasn't listening. He was looking down at the Doctor. 'What's happened to him?'

'I don't know,' said Polly. She came closer.

The Doctor's head was slumped forward, his eyes open. 'He seemed to faint when you came through that door.'

Ben bent down and snapped his fingers in front of the Doctor's face. 'Hey, Doc. Come on. Wakey wakey. It's all right now—it's all over.'

His words seemed to rouse the Doctor. He slowly stirred and raised his eyebrows. 'What? ... What did you say? It's all over? Is that what you said?'

He shook his head. His eyes gazed past Ben—it was as though he was seeing ahead a great way into time.

'That's where you're wrong, my boy. It isn't over. It's not over by a long way.'

'What are you on about, Doctor?' said Ben.

For answer, the Doctor stood up. 'We must get back to the TARDIS immediately.'

'Are you all right, Doctor?' said Polly.

The Doctor shook off her supporting arm. 'We must go now.'

'What's the hurry?' asked Ben. 'Mondas has broken up. There's nothing more to fear from the Cybermen. Aren't we going to go back to the South Pole base to say good-bye?'

The Doctor shook his head impatiently. 'No, no. We must go, I say.' The Doctor drew his borrowed parka around him and hurried out through the door.

'What's happened to him?' Polly looked at Ben.

'Search me! He doesn't seem to know where he is.'

Polly shivered. 'Please Ben, let's get out of here.'

They trudged across towards the TARDIS, now half snowed up. The wind had died; the moon was casting a luminous glow over the gleaming Polar wastes.

Polly paused for a minute. Ahead of them they could see the Doctor trudging through the last few yards of snow to the door of the TARDIS. Polly looked around. The drifting snow had completely covered the dead bodies of the Cybermen. The Polar scene had an incredible purity and innocence—like a dream landscape.

'It's beautiful here,' said Polly. 'I don't suppose we'll ever see it again.'

'We'll become part of it if we don't keep moving! Come on, Duchess.'

He grabbed Polly's arm and led her on towards the TARDIS. The Doctor had already opened the door and walked inside.

As Ben and Polly entered and began stripping off

their furs, there was no sign of the Doctor. They went through into the TARDIS' equipment room, and hung up their heavy International Space Control parkas.

'We should really return these, you know,' said Polly, practical as ever.

Ben shrugged his shoulders. 'I reckon we've earned them. Anyway, they've got ours!' His face looked set and preoccupied. Polly peered at him anxiously.

'Aren't you glad to be back inside here?' said Polly. 'I never thought I'd get so used to this place that I'd call it home! But, after the last few hours, it seems like paradise.'

She turned to walk out into the main TARDIS Control room—but Ben stopped her: 'Half a mo', Duchess. It's the Doctor. I don't think he'll last much longer.'

Polly turned a little pale. 'What do you mean?'

'Haven't you noticed? He's put on a score of years during the last few hours. How old did he say he was once? Hundreds of years? Looking at him now, I'm inclined to believe every day of it!'

Polly shook her head despairingly. 'What can we do?'

'That's just it,' said Ben. 'There's not much we can do, except ...'

Suddenly, a long wailing cry came from the control room. The voice was not the Doctor's.

They rushed out.

They hurried over to a long couch-like arrangement with a folding metal cover over it. The use of it had never been fully explained to them. The Doctor had simply told them that it compressed sleep. The cry seemed to be coming from this apparatus.

'How does it work?' said Polly, struggling with the catch.

Ben pulled back her hand. 'Let me, Duchess.' He turned and pulled down a lever standing beside the apparatus. The hood slid silently back to reveal the long stretcher-like couch.

To their relief, they saw the Doctor's familiar cloak and body. The corner of the long cloak was drawn over his face.

'He's been sleeping,' said Polly, relieved. 'Using the sleeping compressor.'

But Ben was staring at something.

'Hold on, Poll. Look!' He pointed at the Doctor's hands, which were folded over his chest. The Doctor had long, thin, sensitive, rather boney hands. Of late, they had become white and transparent, the blue veins showing through the skin: the hands of a very old man.

But Ben was pointing in amazement at two completely different ones. They were shorter, thicker set, reddish—the hands of a much younger man.

Polly drew back, hand to mouth. 'Oh Ben! Do you think...'

'We'll see,' said Ben grimly. He reached forward gingerly and pulled back the edge of the cloak. The face under the cloak was not the Doctor's. It was the face of a much younger man—a man in his early forties. The Doctor's long, silver locks had been replaced by short dark hair, and the newcomer had a swarthy, almost gypsy, appearance.

As Ben and Polly drew back aghast, the man slowly opened his eyes and turned to looked at them.

'Hello,' he said. His eyes were blue-green—like the sea. Although friendly, they had an elusive, slightly mocking quality. 'You must be Ben and Polly?' he continued.

Ben nodded.

'And who are you?' asked Polly boldly.

The man stretched himself and swung his legs over the edge of the cradle. He stood up and looked down at his hands and legs with a certain pleasurable satisfaction.

'Hum!' he said. 'Not bad!' He flexed his arms. 'Not bad at all.' He turned to Polly. 'You haven't got a mirror by any chance?'

Polly looked at him in amazement. The one thing the old Doctor never had any time for was mirrors. The only mirror on the TARDIS was, in fact, a small, battered metal one in her back pocket. She drew it out and handed it over.

The man took the mirror and held it up. He examined his face. 'Yes,' he said. 'Pretty fair, all told!' He nodded and smiled pleasantly. 'I think I'm going to rather like it.'

'You didn't answer her question,' said Ben, plucking up courage and moving forward, his fists bunched. 'Who the heck are you? And what are you doing here?'

The stranger looked at him in slight surprise. 'You ask me that, Ben? Don't you recognise me?'

The Doctor's two companions shook their heads.

'I thought it was quite obvious,' Again, he smiled his gently mocking smile and winked at them with his blue-green eyes. 'Allow me to introduce myself then. I am the *new* Doctor!'

'DOCTOR WHO'

0426118936	PHILIP HINCHCLIFFE **Doctor Who and The** **Masque of Mandragora**	**85p**
0426201329	TERRANCE DICKS **Doctor Who and The** **Monster of Peladon**	**85p**
0426116909	**Doctor Who and The** **Mutants**	**£1.25**
0426201302	**Doctor Who and The** **Nightmare of Eden**	**85p**
0426112520	**Doctor Who and The** **Planet of the Daleks**	**£1.25**
042610997X	**Doctor Who and The** **Revenge of the Cybermen**	**95p**
0426200616	**Doctor Who and The** **Robots of Death**	**90p**
0426200497	IAN MARTER **Doctor Who and the Sontaren** **Experiment**	**£1.25**
0426110331	MALCOLM HULKE **Doctor Who and The** **Space War**	**85p**
0426200993	TERRANCE DICKS **Doctor Who and The** **Stones of Blood**	**95p**
0426119738	**Doctor Who and The** **Talons of Weng Chaing**	**£1.25**
0426110684	GERRY DAVIS **Doctor Who and The** **Tenth Planet**	**85p**
0426115007	TERRANCE DICKS **Doctor Who and The** **Terror of the Autons**	**75p**

Prices are subject to alteration

'DOCTOR WHO'

0426200373	TERRANCE DICKS **Doctor Who and The Android Invasion**	**90p**
0426201086	**Doctor Who and the Androids of Tara**	**75p**
0426201043	**Doctor Who and The Armageddon Factor**	**85p**
0426116313	IAN MARTER **Doctor Who and The Ark in Space**	**90p**
0426116747	**Doctor Who and The Brain of Morbius**	**95p**
0426117034	TERRANCE DICKS **Doctor Who and The Claws of Axos**	**75p**
042620123X	DAVID FISHER **Doctor Who and The Creature from the Pit**	**90p**
0426114981	BRIAN HAYLES **Doctor Who and The Curse of Peladon**	**75p**
0426114639	GERRY DAVIS **Doctor Who and The Cybermen**	**85p**
0426113322	BARRY LETTS **Doctor Who and The Daemons**	**£1.50**
0426101103	DAVID WHITAKER **Doctor Who and The Daleks**	**85p**
042611244X	TERRANCE DICKS **Doctor Who and The Dalek Invasion of Earth**	**£1.25**
0426103807	**Doctor Who and The Day of the Daleks**	**85p**

Prices are subject to alteration

STAR Books are obtainable from many booksellers and newsagents. If you have any difficulty please send purchase price plus postage on the scale below to:

Star Cash Sales
P.O. Box 11
Falmouth
Cornwall
OR
Star Book Service,
G.P.O. Box 29,
Douglas,
Isle of Man,
British Isles.

While every effort is made to keep prices low, it is sometimes necessary to increase prices at short notice. Star Books reserve the right to show new retail prices on covers which may differ from those advertised in the text or elsewhere.

Postage and Packing Rate
UK: 40p for the first book, 18p for the second book and 13p for each additional book ordered to a maximum charge of £1·49p. BFPO and EIRE: 40p for the first book, 18p for the second book, 13p per copy for the next 7 books, thereafter 7p per book. Overseas: 60p for the first book and 18p per copy for each additional book.